No one **writes romantic** fiction like Barbara Cartland.

Miss Cartland was originally inspired by the best of the romantic novelists she read as a girl —writers such as Elinor Glyn, Ethel M. Dell and E. M. Hull. Convinced that her own wide audience would also delight in her favorite authors, Barbara Cartland has taken their classic tales of romance and specially adapted them for today's readers.

Bantam is proud to publish these novels—personally selected and edited by Miss Cartland— under the imprint

BARBARA CARTLAND'S LIBRARY OF LOVE

Bantam Books by Barbara Cartland
Ask your bookseller for the books you have missed

Barbara Cartland's Library of Love

Barbara Cartland's Library of Love
The Price of Things
by Elinor Glyn

Condensed by Barbara Cartland

BANTAM BOOKS
TORONTO · NEW YORK · LONDON

THE PRICE OF THINGS
A Bantam Book / June 1978

Bantam Books are published by Bantam Books, Inc. Its trade-
mark, consisting of the words "Bantam Books" and the por-
trayal of a bantam, is registered in the United States Patent
Office and in other countries. Marca Registrada. Bantam
Books, Inc., 666 Fifth Avenue, New York, New York 10019.

Introduction
by
Barbara Cartland

This is one of Elinor Glyn's novels which compels one to keep reading in case there is not the happy ending for which one longs.

The characters are clear-cut, definite, and decisive. I love and could never forget the gentle Amaryllis and the handsome, passionate Denzil. I trembled at what the evil Harietta might do to them. I know you will feel the same.

Chapter
One

"If one consciously and deliberately desires happiness on this plane," said the Russian, "one must have sufficient strength of will to banish all thought."

"What do you mean by 'thought'? How can one not think?"

Amaryllis Ardayre's large grey eyes opened in a puzzled way.

She was on her honeymoon in Paris and for the moment at a party at the Russian Embassy, and until now she had accepted things and not speculated about them.

She was accepting her honeymoon with her accustomed calm, although it was not causing her any of the thrills which Elsie Goldmore, her school friend, had assured her she should discover therein.

Honeymoons! Heavens! But perhaps it was because Sir John was dull. He looked dull, she thought, as he stood there talking to the Ambassador. A fine figure of an Englishman, but yes, dull.

The Russian, on the contrary, was not dull.

He was huge and ugly and rough-hewn, his eyes were yellowish green and slanted upwards, and his face was frankly Calmuck.

"How can one not think?" Amaryllis Ardayre asked again. "I am always thinking."

"Oh no, you are not," he smiled indulgently, "you only imagine that you are. You have questioned nothing, you do right generally because you have a nice character and have been well brought up, not because of any conscious determination to uplift the soul. Yes? Is it not so?"

She was startled.

"Perhaps."

"Do you ever ask yourself what things mean? What we are? Where we are going? What is the end of it all? No, you are happy, you live from day to day."

She was not accustomed to discuss unorthodox subjects, but she was interested, and told him so.

After a pause, Amaryllis Ardayre looked at the crowds passing and repassing in those stately rooms.

"Tell me, who is that woman over there?" she asked. "The very pretty one with the fair hair and wearing jade-green. She looks radiantly happy."

"And is. She is, frankly, an animal, exquisitely preserved, damnably selfish, completely devoid of intellect, and with sugary manners and the senses of a harem houri—and the tenacity of a rat."

"You are severe."

"Not at all. Harietta Boleski is a very selfish woman."

"Boleski . . . that is a Russian name, is it not?"

"No, Polish. She secured our Stanislass, a

great man in his country, last year in Berlin, having divorced a no longer required but worthy German husband, who had held some post in the American Consulate there."

"Is that old man standing obediently beside her your Stanislass? He looks quite cowed."

"A sad sight, is it not? Stanislass, though, is not old, barely forty. He had a *béguin* for her. She put his intelligence to sleep and bamboozled his judgement with a continuous appeal to the senses; she has vampired him now.

"She rules and eats his soul as she has done to the souls of others. Shall I present her to you? As a type, she is worthy of your attention."

Amaryllis shuddered.

"It sounds as if she has the evil eye, as the Italians say."

"Only for men. She is really an amiable creature; women like her. She is so frankly simple, since for her there are never two issues—only to be allowed her own desires, a riot of extravagance, in the first place, and someone to gratify certain instincts without too many refinements when the mood takes her.

"For the rest, she is kind and good-natured and 'jolly,' as you English say, and has no notion that she is a road to hell. But they are mostly dead, her other spider-mates, and cannot tell of it."

"I am much interested. I should like to talk to her."

Madame Boleski swept towards them on the arm of an Austrian Prince, and the Russian, Verischenzko, said with suave politeness:

"*Madame,* let me present you to Lady Ardayre. With me she has been admiring you from afar."

The two women curtseyed, and with cheery, disarming simplicity Harietta Boleski made some gracious remarks in a voice which sounded as if she smoked too much; but it was not disagreeable in tone, nor had she a pronounced accent.

"So delighted to meet you," she said. "We are going over to London next month and I am just crazy to know more of you delicious English people."

They chatted for a few moments and then *Madame* Boleski swept onwards. She was quite stately and graceful and had a well-posed head.

Amaryllis turned to the Russian and was startled by the expression of fierce, sardonic amusement in his yellow-green eyes.

"But surely she can see that you are laughing at her?" she exclaimed in astonishment.

"It would convey nothing to her if she did."

"But you looked positively wicked."

"Possibly. I feel it sometimes when I think of Stanislass; he was a very good friend of mine."

Sir John Ardayre joined them at this moment and the three walked towards the supper-room, then the Russian said good-night.

"It is not good-bye, *Madame.* I too shall be in your country soon, and I hope I may see you again before you leave Paris."

They arranged a dinner for the following night but one, and said *au revoir*.

An hour later the Russian was seated in a huge English leather chair in the little salon of his *appartement* in the Rue Cambon, when *Madame* Boleski very softly entered the room and sat down upon his knee.

"I had to come, darling brute," she said. "I was jealous of the English girl."

She fitted her delicately painted lips to his.

"Stanislass wanted to talk over his new scheme for Poland too, and as you know that always gets on my nerves."

But Verischenzko threw his head back impatiently, while he answered roughly:

"I am not in the mood for your chastisement tonight. Go back as you came. I am thinking of something real, something which makes your body of no use to me; it wearies me and I do not even desire your presence. Be gone!"

Then he kissed her neck insolently and pushed her off his knee.

She pouted resentfully. But suddenly her eyes caught a small case lying on a table near, and an eager gleam came into their hazel depths.

"Oh, Stépan! It is the ruby ring! Oh, you beloved angel, you are going to give it to me after all! Oh, now I'll rush off at once and leave you, if you wish it! Good-night!"

*   *   *

"What are you doing in Paris, Denzil?"

"I came over for a bit of racing. Awfully glad to see you—can't we dine together? I go back tomorrow."

Verischenzko put his arm through Denzil Ardayre's and drew him into the Café de Paris, at the door of which they had chanced to meet.

"I had another guest, but she can be consoled with some of Midas's food, and I want to talk to you. Were you going to eat alone?"

"A fellow threw me over. I meant to have just a snack and go on to a theatre. It is good running across you; I thought you were miles away!"

Verischenzko spoke to the head waiter, and gave him directions as to the disposal of the lovely lady who would presently arrive, and then he went

on to his table, rather at the top, in a fairly secluded corner.

The few people who were already dining—it
was early on this May night—looked at Denzil
Ardayre.

He was such a refreshing sight of health and
youth, so tall and fit and English, with his brown,
smooth head and fearless, blue eyes, gay and debonair.

One could see that he played cricket and polo,
and any other game that came along, and that not
a muscle of his frame was out of condition.

They talked for a while of casual things, and
then Verischenzko said:

"Some relations of yours are here, Sir John
Ardayre and his particularly attractive bride. Shall
we eat what I had ordered for Collette, or have
you other fancies after the soup?"

Denzil only paid attention to the first part of
the speech. He looked surprised and interested.

"John Ardayre here! Of course, he married
about ten days ago; he is the head of the family,
as you are aware, but I hardly even know him by
sight. He is quite ten years older than I am and
does not trouble about us, the poor younger
branch. . . ."

He smiled, showing such good teeth.

"Besides, as you know, I have been for such
a long time in India, and the leaves were for sport,
not for hunting up relations."

"I want to hear all that you know about
them," Verischenzko said. "The girl is an exquisite
thing with immense possibilities. Sir John looks—
dull."

"He is really a splendid character though,"
Denzil hastened to assure him. "Do you know the
family history? But no, of course not; we were

too busy in the old days enjoying life to trouble to talk of such things!

"Well, it is rather strange. In the last generation things very nearly came to an end, but John has built it all up again. You are interested in heredity?"

"Naturally—what is the story?"

"Our mutual great-grandfather was a tremendous personage in North Somerset; the Ardayre place is there. My father was the son of the younger son, who had just enough to do him decently at Eton and enable him to scrape along in the old regiment with a pony or two to play with.

"My mother was a Willowbrook, as you know, and a considerable heiress; that's how I come out all right. But until John's father, Sir James, squandered things, the head of the family was always very rich and awfully set on the dignity of his race."

"The father of this man made a *gaspillage*, then—well?"

"Yes, he was a rotter, a hark-back to his mother's relations. She was a Cranmote, and they ruin any blood they mix with. I am glad that I come from the generation before."

Denzil helped himself to a Russian salad, and went on leisurely:

"He fortunately married Lady Mary de la Paule, who was a saint, and so John seems to have righted, and takes after her. She died quite early; she had had enough of Sir James, I expect. He had gambled away everything he could lay hands upon.

"Poor John was brought up with a tutor at home, for some reason—hard luck on a man. He was only about thirteen when she died, and at seventeen went straight into the city. He was determined to make a fortune, it has always been said, and redeem the mortgages on Ardayre—very splendid of him, wasn't it?"

"Yes, well, all this is not out of the ordinary line. What comes next?"

Denzil laughed.

"The poor lady was no sooner dead than the old boy married a Bulgarian snake-charmer, whom he had picked up in Constantinople! You may well smile!"

Verischenzko had raised his eyebrows in a whimsical way; this did sound such a highly coloured incident!

"It was an unusual sort of thing to do, I admit, but the tale grows more lurid still, when I tell you that five months after the wedding she produced a son by the Lord knows who, one of her own tribe probably!

"And old Sir James was so infatuated with her that he never protested, and presently when he and John quarrelled like hell, he pretended the little brute was his own child, just to spite John."

Verischenzko's eyes narrowed.

"And does this result of the fusion of the snake-charmer figure in the family history? I believe I have met him—his name is Ferdinand, is it not? And he is, or was, in some business in Constantinople."

"That is the creature. He was brought up at Ardayre as though he were the heir, and poor John turned out of things. Ferdinand came to Eton three years before I left, but even there they could not turn him into the outside semblance of a gentleman.

"I loathed the little toad and he loathed me, and the sickening part of the thing is that if John does not have a son, by the English law of entail Ferdinand will come into Ardayre and become the head of the family."

He paused before continuing:

"Old Sir James died about five years ago, always protesting that this bastard was his own child, though everyone knew it was a lie. However, by that time John had made enough in the city to redeem Ardayre twice over.

"He had tremendous luck after the South African War, so he came into possession and lives there now in great state. I do really hope he will have a son."

"You too have the instinct of the family, then, this pride in it, since it cannot benefit you either way."

"I believe it is born in us, and though I have never seen the Ardayre estate, I should hate this mongrel to have it. I was brought up with a tremendous reverence for it, even as a second cousin."

"Well, the new Lady Ardayre looks young enough and of a health to have ten sons!"

"Yes . . ." Denzil acquiesced in a tentative tone.

"Not so?"

Verischenzko glanced up, surprised, and then gave his attention to the waiter who had brought some burgundy and was pouring it into his glass.

"Not so, you would say?"

"I don't know, I have never seen her, but in the family it is whispered that John, poor devil —he had an accident hunting two or three years ago; however, it may not any of it be true. Here, let us drink to the Ardayre son!"

"To the Ardayre son!"

Verischenzko filled his friend's glass with the decanted wine and they both drank together.

"Your cousin is like you," the Russian said presently. "A fatiguing likeness, but the same height and make and voice. Strange things, these family reproductions of an exact type. I have no family, as you know; we are of the people, risen by trade to riches.

"Could I go beyond my immediate parents, could I know cousins and uncles and brothers, should I find this same peculiar stamp of family among us all? Who knows? I think not."

"I suppose there is something in that. My father has told me that in the picture gallery at Ardayre they are as like as two pins the whole way down."

Then, as Denzil would have continued, Verischenzko hastily asked:

"Will you dine tomorrow night at the Ritz to meet your cousin and his wife? They are honouring me."

"I wish I could, but I am off in the morning. What is she like?"

Verischenzko paid particular attention to the selection of a quail, then he answered:

"She is of the same type as the family, Denzil —that is, a good skeleton, bones in the right place, firm white flesh, the same colouring as yours, well bred, balanced, unawakened as yet. Was she a relation?"

"Yes, I believe so—a cousin of a generation even before mine. I wish I could dine with you; I would very much like to meet them, so I shall have to make a chance in England.

"It is stupid not to know one's own family, but our fathers quarrelled and we have never had a chance of mending the break."

"They were at the Russian Embassy last night, and the throng admired Lady Ardayre very much."

"And what are you doing in Paris, Stépan? The last I heard of you, you were on your yacht in the Black Sea."

"I was cruising near countries whose internal affairs interested me for the moment. I returned to my *appartement* in Paris to see a friend of mine, Stanislass Boleski."

At that moment Stanislass and his wife, Harietta, entered.

Denzil looked at her with interest.

"Who did you say her first husband was?" Denzil asked after a few moments.

"A German by the name of Von Wendel. He used to beat her with a stick, it is said, so naturally such a nature as hers adored Stanislass. I did not meet her until she had got rid of Von Wendel and he had disappeared. She would sacrifice anyone who stood in her way."

"Your friend, the present husband, looks pretty *épuisée;* one feels sorry for the poor man."

Then, as ever at the mention of the *débâcle* of Stanislass, Verischenzko's eyes filled with a fierce light.

"She has crushed the hope of Poland, and for that, indeed, one day she must pay."

"But I thought you Russians did not greatly love the Poles?" Denzil remarked.

"Enlightened Russians can see beyond their old prejudices, and Stanislass was a lifetime friend. One day a new dawn will come for our northern world."

Afterwards, as they went out, they passed close by the Boleskis, and the two rose and spoke to Verischenzko with *empressement.*

He introduced Captain Ardayre and talked for a few minutes, then they said good-night and went out.

But as Stépan passed, a man, half-hidden behind a pillar, leaned forward and looked at him, and in his light blue eyes there burned a jealous hate.

"Ah, *Gott in Himmel!*" he growled to himself. "It is he whom she loves, not the pig-fool whom we gave her to. One day I shall kill him!" And he raised his glass of Rhine wine and murmured, *"Der Tag!"*

* * *

That evening Sir John Ardayre had taken his bride to dine in the Bois, and they were sitting listening to the Tziganes at Armenonville. Amaryllis was conscious that the evening lacked something.

The circumstances were interesting: a bride of ten days, and the environment so illuminating, and yet there was John, smoking an expensive cigar and not saying *anything!* She did not like people who chattered, and she could even imagine a delicious silence wrought with meaning.

But a stolid, respectable silence with Tziganes playing moving airs and the romantic background of this joyous Parisian out-of-doors night-life surely demanded some show of emotion!

John loved her, she supposed; of course he did, or he never would have asked her to marry him, rich as he was and poor as she had been.

She could not help going over all their acquaintance; the date of its beginning was only three months back!

They had met at a country house and had played golf together, then they had met again a month later at another house, in March, but she could not remember any love-making.

She could not recall any of those warm looks and surreptitious hand-clasps when the occasion was propitious, which Elsie Goldmore had told her men were so prodigal in demonstrating when they fell in love.

Indeed, she had seen emotion upon the faces of quite two or three young men, for all her secluded life and restricted means, since she had left the school in Dresden, where a worldly maiden aunt had sent her.

German officers there had looked at her with interest in the street, and the clergyman's three sons and the Squire's two, when she returned home.

Indeed, Tom Clarke had gone further than that!

He had kissed her cheek while coming out the door in the dark one evening, and had received a severe rebuff for his pains.

She had read quantities of novels, ancient and modern. She knew that love was a wonderful thing; she knew also that modern life and its exigencies had created a new and far more matter-of-fact point of view about love than that which one obtained from most books.

She did not expect much, and had indulged in none of those visions of romantic bliss which girls were once supposed to spend their time in constructing.

But she did expect *something,* and here was nothing, just nothing!

The day John had asked her to marry him he had not been much moved. He had put the question to her simply and calmly, and she had not dreamed of refusing him.

It was obviously her duty, and it had always been her intention to marry well, if the chance came her way, and so leave a not too congenial home.

She had been to a few London Balls with her aunt, a personage of some prestige and character. But invitations did not flow to a penniless young woman from the country, nor did partners flock to be presented to strangers in these days, and Amaryllis had spent many humiliating hours as a wallflower and had grown to hate Balls.

She was not expansive, did not make friends easily, and, pretty as she was, as a girl, luck did not come her way.

When she had said yes in as matter-of-fact a voice as the proposal of marriage had been made to her, Sir John had replied, "You are a dear," and that had seemed to her a most ordinary remark.

He had leaned over—they were climbing a steep pitch in search of a fugitive golf-ball—and taken her hand respectfully, and then he had kissed her forehead, or her ear, she forgot which—nothing that mattered much or gave her any thrill!

"I hope I shall make you happy," he had added. "I am a dull sort of a fellow, but I will try."

Then they had talked of the usual things that they talked about every day, and then had returned to the house; and by the evening everyone knew of the engagement, and she was congratulated on all sides and petted by the hostess.

She and John were left ostentatiously alone in a smaller drawing-room after dinner, and there was not a grain of excitement in the whole conventional thing!

There was always a shadow too in John's

blue eyes. He was the most reserved creature in this world, she supposed.

That might be all very well, but what was the good of being so reserved with the woman you liked well enough to make your wife, if it made you never able to get beyond talking on general subjects?

This she had asked herself many times, and had determined to break down the reserve. But John never changed; he was always considerate and polite and perfectly at ease.

He would talk quietly and with common sense to whomever he was placed next to, and very seldom a look of interest flickered in his eyes.

Indeed, Amaryllis had never seen him really interested until he spoke of Ardayre, and then his voice altered tremendously.

He spoke to her of his home often during their engagement, and she grew to know that it was something sacred to him, and that the family and its honour and traditions meant more to him than any individual person could ever mean.

She almost became jealous of it all.

Her trousseau was quite nice, her aunt had seen to that, and Amaryllis felt triumphant as she walked up the aisle of St. George's Hanover Square.

Everyone was so pleased about the wedding. An Ardayre married to an Ardayre! Good blood on both sides, and everything suitable and rich and prosperous, and just as it should be!

And there stood her handsome, stolid bridegroom, serenely calm, and the white flowers, and the Bishop, and her silver brocade train, and the pages, and the bridesmaids. Oh yes, a wedding was a most agreeable thing!

And could she have penetrated into the thoughts of John Ardayre, she would have heard as he knelt there beside her at the altar rail:

"O God, keep the axe from falling yet: give me a son."

The most curious emotions of excitement rose in her when they went off in the smart new automobile *en route* to that inevitable country house "lent by the bridegroom's uncle, the Earl de la Paule, for the first days of the honeymoon."

This particular mansion was on the river, only two hours' drive from her aunt's Charles Street door.

Now that she was his wife, surely John would begin to make love to her, real love!

For Elsie Goldmore had presumed upon their schoolgirl friendship and been quite explicit in these last days, and in any case Amaryllis was not a Miss of the Victorian era. The feminine world has grown too unrefined in the expression of its private affairs and too indiscreet for any maiden to remain in ignorance now.

It is true that John did kiss her once or twice, but there was no real warmth in the embrace, and when after an excellent dinner her heart began to beat with wonderment and excitement, she asked herself what it meant.

Then, all confused, she murmured something about "good-night" and retired to the magnificent state suite alone.

When she had left him, John Ardayre drank down a full glass of Benedictine and followed her up the stairs. But there was no lover's exaltation; there was only an anguish almost of despair in his eyes.

Amaryllis thought of that night, and of other

nights since, as she sat there at Armenonville, in the luminous, sensuous dusk.

So this was being married! Well, it was not much of a joy; and why, why did John sit there silently? Why?

Surely this is not how the Russian would have sat! That strange Russian!

Chapter
Two

The day after the wonderful rejoicing, of which the home-coming of Amaryllis had been the occasion at Ardayre, she was sitting, waiting for her husband, in that exquisite cedar parlour which led from her room.

They would breakfast cosily there, she had arranged, and nothing was wanting in the setting of a love-scene. The bride wore the most alluring cap and daintiest Parisian *négligé,* and her fair, pure skin gleamed through the diaphanous material.

How she longed for John to notice it all and make love to her! She had apprehended a number of delightful possibilities in Paris, none of which had materialised, alas, in her case.

John was the same as ever, quiet, dignified, polite, and unmoved.

She had taken to turning out the light before he came to her at night, to hide the disappointment and chagrin which she felt might show in her eyes. It would be so humiliating if he should see this.

There would soon be nothing left for her to do but pretend that she was as cold as he was, if this last effort at *frou-frous* left him as stolid as usual.

She smoothed out the pale chiffon draperies of her gown with a tender hand, then got up and looked at herself in the mirror.

It was fortunate that the reflection of snowy nose and throat and chin, and the pink velvety cheeks, required no art to perfect them; it was all natural and quite nice, she felt. What a bore it must be to have to touch up like *Madame* Boleski!

However, she would try, oh, try so hard, to entice John to be lovely to her. He was her own husband; there was absolutely no harm in doing this. And how glorious it would be to turn him into a lover, here in this perfectly divine old house!

John was so good-looking, too, and had the most attractive deep voice, but heavens! the matter-of-factness of everything about him!

How long would it all go on?

John came in presently with *The Times* under his arm. He was immaculately dressed in a blue serge suit.

Amaryllis had hoped to see him in that subduedly gorgeous dressing-gown she had persuaded him to order at Charvet's during their first days. It would have been so suitable and intimate and lover-like.

But no, there was the blue serge suit, and *The Times!*

A shadow fell upon her mood. Her own pink chiffons almost seemed out-of-place.

John glanced at them, and at the glowing, living, delicious bit of young womanhood which they adorned.

He saw the rebellious ripe cherry of a mouth and the warm, soft tenderness in the grey eyes; and then he quickly looked out the window, his own blue ones expressionless—but the hand which held the newspaper was clenched rather hard.

"Am I not a pet!" cooed Amaryllis, deliberately subduing the chill of her first disappointment. "Dearest, see, I have kept this last and loveliest set of garments for the morning of our home-coming . . . and for you!"

She crept close to him and laid her cheek against his.

He encircled her with his arm and kissed her calmly.

"You look most beautiful, darling," he said. "But then you always do, and your frills are perfection. Now I think we ought to have breakfast; it is most awfully late."

She sat down in her place and felt stupid tears rise in her eyes. She poured out the tea and buttered herself some toast, while John was apparently busy at a side-table where the hot dishes were.

He selected the daintiest piece of sole for her and handed her the plate.

"I am not hungry," she protested; "keep it for yourself."

He did not press the matter, but took his place and began to talk quietly upon the news of the day, in a composed fashion, between glances at *The Times* and mouthfuls of sole.

Amaryllis controlled herself. She was too proud and too just to make a foolish scene. If this was John's way and her little effort at enticement was a failure, she must just put up with it.

Marriage was a lottery, she had always heard, and it might be her luck to have drawn a blank!

So she choked down the rising emotion and answered brightly, showing interest in her husband's remarks, and she even managed to eat some omelette; and when the business of breakfast was quite over she went to the window.

John followed her there.

The view which met their eyes was exquisite.

Beyond the perfect, stately garden, with its quaint clipped yews and masses of spring flowers and its velvety lawns, there stretched the vast park with its splendid oaks and browsing deer.

It was a possession which any man would feel proud to own.

John slipped his arm round her waist and drew her to him.

"Amaryllis," he said, and his voice vibrated, "today I am going to show you everything I love here at Ardayre, because I want you to love it all too. You are of the family, so it must mean something to you, dear."

Amaryllis kindled with reawakening hope.

"Indeed, it will mean everything to me, John."

He kissed her forehead and murmured something about her dressing quickly, and that he would wait for her there in the cedar room.

And when she returned in about a quarter of an hour, in the neatest country clothes, he placed her hand on his arm and led her down the great stairs, on through the hall, and into the picture gallery.

It was a wonderful place of green silk and chestnut wainscotting, and all the walls of its hundred feet of length were hung with canvasses of value, principally portraits of those Ardayres who had gone on.

Looking down on Amaryllis was face after face of the same type as John's and her own, the brown hair, and the eyes of grey or blue. Some were a little fairer, some a little darker, but all unmistakably stamped "Ardayre."

John pointed out to her each individual, while she hung fondly on his arm, from some doubtful, crude, fourteenth-century wooden panels of Johns and Denzils and on to a Benedict in a furred Henry VII gown.

Then came Henrys and more Denzils in Elizabethan armour and puffed white satin, and through Stewart and Commonwealth to Stewart again, and so to William and Mary numbers of Benedicts, and lastly to powdered Georgian Jameses and Regency Denzils and Johns.

And the name Amaryllis recurred more than once in stately dames and damsels, called after that fair Amaryllis of Elizabeth's days who had been maid-of-honour to the virgin Queen, and had had sonnets written to her nut-brown locks by the gallants of her time.

"How little the women they married seemed to have altered the type!" the young, living Amaryllis exclaimed when they came nearly to the end.

"It goes on Ardayre, Ardayre, Ardayre, ever since the very first one. Oh, John, if we ever have a son he ought to be even more so, you and I being of the same blood. . . ."

And then she hesitated and blushed crimson. This was the first time she had ever spoken of such a thing.

John held her arm very tightly to his side for a second, and his voice was uncertain as he answered:

"Amaryllis, that is the profound desire of my heart, that we should have a son."

A strange feeling of exaltation came over Amaryllis, half innocent and wholly ignorant as she was.

"Oh . . . darling, when . . . when do you think we shall have a son?"

Then for the first time in their lives John Ardayre clasped her in his arms passionately and held her to his heart.

"Ah, God," he whispered hoarsely, as he kissed her fresh young lips. "Pray for that, Amaryllis; pray for that, my own."

Then he restrained himself and drew her on to the last four pictures at the end of the room. They were of his grandfather and grandmother and his father and mother.

Then there was a blank space, and the brighter colour of the damask showed that a canvass had been removed.

Who hung there, John?"

"The accursed snake-charmer woman whom my father disgraced the family with by bringing home; she was his wife by law. A Frenchman painted her and it was a fine picture, with the bastard Ferdinand in her arms, the proof of our shame. I had it taken down and burnt the day the place was mine."

Amaryllis was receiving surprises today. John's face was full of emotion, his eyes sparkling with hate as he spoke.

How he must love everything connected with his home, and its honour, and its name; he could not be so very cold after all!

When lunch-time came, the usual relations of obvious and commonplace good fellowship had been fully restored between them, and that atmosphere of aloofness which seemed impossible to banish had enveloped John once more.

Amaryllis sighed, but it was too soon to despair, she thought, after the hope of John's words; and with her serene temperament she decided to leave things as they were for the present, and trust to time.

But as her maid brushed out her soft brown hair that night, an unrest and a longing for something came over her again: what, she knew not, nor could have put it into words.

She let herself relive that moment when John had pressed her with passion to his heart. Perhaps . . . perhaps that was the beginning of a change in him? Perhaps . . . presently . . .

But the clock in the long gallery had chimed two, and there was yet no sound of John in the dressing-room beyond.

Amaryllis lay in the great splendid gilt bed in the warm darkness, and at last tears trickled down her cheeks.

What could keep him so long away from her? Why did he not come?

The large Queen Anne windows were wide open and soft noises of the night floated in with the zephyrs. The whole air seemed filled with waiting expectancy for something tender and passionate to be.

What was that? Steps upon the terrace, measured steps, and then silence, and then a deep sigh.

It must be John, out there alone! When she would love to have stayed with him, to have woven sweet fancies in the luminous darkness, to have taken and given long kisses, to have buried her face in the honeysuckle which grew there, steeped in dew.

But he had said to her after their stately dinner in the great dining-hall:

"Play to me a little, Amaryllis, and then go to bed, child, for you must be tired out."

And after that he had not spoken more, but pushed her gently towards the door, with a solemn kiss on the forehead and just a murmured "good-night."

And she had deceived herself and thought that it meant he would come quickly, and so she had run up the stairs.

But now it was after two in the morning and would soon be growing towards dawn, and John was out there sighing alone!

She crept to the window and leaned upon the sill. She thought that she could distinguish his tall figure there by the carved stone bench.

"John!" she called softly. "I am so lonely ... John dearest ... won't you come?"

Then she felt that her ears must be deceiving her, for there was the sound of a faint, suppressed sob; and then, a second afterwards, her husband's voice answered cheerily, with its usual casual note:

"You naughty little night-bird! Go back to bed and to sleep. Yes, I am coming immediately now."

But when he did steal in silently from the dressing-room an hour later, in the grey dawn, Amaryllis, worn out from speculation and disappointment, had fallen asleep.

He looked down upon her charming face, the long, curly brown lashes sweeping her flushed cheeks, and at the rounded, beautiful, girlish form, all his very own, to clasp and to kiss and to hold in his arms.

Two scalding tears gathered in his blue eyes, and he took his place beside her without making a sound.

*   *   *

"Here are the papers, Hans, but I think the whole thing is stupid nonsense. What does it matter to anyone what Poland wants? What a nuisance all these old boring political things are!

"They always spoilt our happiness since the

beginning, and now if it weren't for them we could have a glorious time here together. I would love managing to come out to meet you under Stanislass's nose. None of the others I have ever had is as good in the way of a lover as you are."

The man swore in German under his breath.

"Of a lightness always, Harietta! No *dévouement,* no patriotism. . . ! Should I have agreed to the divorce, loving your body as I do, had it not been a serious matter? The pig-dog who now owns you must be sucked dry of information, and then I shall take you back again."

A cunning look came into *Madame* Boleski's hazel eyes. She had not the slightest intention of permitting this.

To go back to Hans, to the difficulty of making both ends meet, even though he did cause every inch of her well-preserved body to tingle!

They had suggested her getting the divorce for their own stupid political ends, to be able to place her in the arms of Stanislass Boleski, and there she meant to stay!

However, at the moment she wanted Hans, the man, and was determined to waste no further time on useless discussion.

So she began her blandishments, taking pride in showing him her beautiful garments and her string of big pearls; each thing exhibited between her voluptuous kisses, until Hans grew intoxicated with desire and became as clay in her hands.

"It is not your pig-dog of a husband I wish to kill!" he said, after one hour had gone by in inarticulate murmurings. "Him I do not fear, it is the Russian, Verischenzko, who fills me with hate.

"We have regard of him, he does not go unobserved; and if you allure him also among the rest, beyond the instructions which you were given, then there will be unpleasantness for you, my little cat; your Hans will twist his bear's neck, and yours also if need be!"

"Verischenzko!" Harietta laughed. "Why, I hardly know him; he doesn't amount to a row of pins! He's Stanislass's friend, not mine."

After some more fierce caresses had come to an end—there was no delicacy about Harietta— Hans continued his discourse:

"There has come here to Paris a young man by the name of Ardayre, Ferdinand Ardayre. He is slippery but he can be of the greatest value to us. See that you become friends.

"He hates his brother, who is the head of the family, and he hates his brother's wife for family reasons which it is not necessary to waste time in telling you. I knew him in Constantinople. Underneath, I believe, he hates the English; there is a slur on him. . . ."

"I have already met him," Harietta said, her eyes sparkling. "I hate the wife also, for my own reasons. Yes; how can I help you with this?"

"It is Ferdinand you must concentrate on. I am not concerned with the brother or his wife, except insofar as his hate for them can be used to our advantage. Do not embark upon this to play games of your own for your hate; you may become foolish then and upset matters."

"Very well." The two objectives could go together, Harietta felt; she never wasted words. It would be a pleasure one day, perhaps, to be able to injure that girl whom Verischenzko certainly respected, if he was not actually growing to love her.

Seven o'clock struck. She had thoroughly enjoyed being with Hans; he satisfied her in many ways, and it was also a relaxation, as she need not act.

But the joys of the interview were over now, and she had others prepared for later on, and must go back to the Rhin to dress.

So she kissed Hans and left, having arranged to meet him on the following Tuesday night here in his rooms, and having received precise instructions as to the nature of the information to be obtained from Ferdinand Ardayre.

Life would be Paradise if only it were not for these ridiculous and tiresome political intrigues. Harietta had no taste for actual intrigue, and its intricacies were a weariness to her.

If she could have married a rich man in the beginning, she always told herself, she would never have mixed herself up in anything of this kind; and now that she *had* married a rich man, she would try to get out of the nuisance as soon as possible.

Meanwhile, there was Ferdinand, and Ferdinand was falling in love with her.

"He'll be no difficulty," she told herself with a sigh of relief.

It would not be as it had been with Verischenzko, whom she had been directed to capture. For in Verischenzko she had found a master, not a dupe.

When she reached the beautiful Champs-Élysées she looked at her diamond wrist-watch. It was only ten minutes past seven, and the dinner at the Austrian Embassy was not until half-past eight.

Dressing was a serious business to Harietta, but she meant to cut it down to half-an-hour tonight, because there was a certain *appartement* in the Rue Cambon which she intended to visit for a few minutes.

"What an original street to have an *appartement* in!" people always said to Verischenzko.

"Nothing but business houses and modest hotels for travellers!"

And the shabby-looking *porte cochère* gave no evidence of the old Louis XV mansion within, converted now into a series of offices, all but the top floor looking on to the gardens of the *Ministère*.

Verischenzko, having taken it for its situation and its isolation, had converted it into a thing of great beauty, with panelling and rare pictures and the most comfortable chairs.

Madame Boleski leisurely ascended the shallow stairs—there was no lift—and rang her three short rings, which Peter, the Russian servant, was accustomed to expect.

The door was opened at once and she was taken through the quaint square hall and into the master's own sitting-room, a richly sombre place of oak *boiserie* and old crimson silk.

Verischenzko was writing, and just glanced up while he murmured Napoleon's famous order to *Mademoiselle* George, but Harietta Boleski pushed out her full underlip and sat down in a deep armchair.

"No, not this evening, I have only a moment. I have merely come, Stépan, you darling, to tell you that I have something interesting to say."

"Not possible!"

He carefully sealed the letter he had been writing and put it ready to be posted.

"You have come not for pleasure but to talk! *Sapristi!* I am truly amazed!"

Another woman would have been insulted by the tone of his voice and the insinuation in his words, but not so Harietta.

She did not pretend to have a brain—that was one of her strong points—and she understood and appreciated the crudest methods, so long as their end was for the pleasure of herself.

She nodded, and that was all.

Verischenzko threw himself into the chair opposite hers, his yellow-green eyes full of a mocking light.

"I have seen a brooch at Cartier's just now even finer than the ruby ring I gave you recently; I thought that perhaps if I was very pleased with you, it might be yours."

Harietta bounded from her chair and sat upon his knee.

"You perfect angel, Stépan! I adore you!" she said.

He did not return the caresses at all, but just ordered:

"Now talk."

She spoke rapidly and he listened intently; he was weighing her words and searching for their truth.

He decided that, for some reason of her own, she was not lying, and in any case it did not matter if she was or was not, because he had resources at his command which would enable him to test the information, and if it was true it would be worth the brooch.

'Who is her German correspondent? This I must discover, but since this is the first time she has knowingly given me information, it proves that there is some revenge in her goat's brain. Now is the time to obtain the most.'

He encircled her with his arm and kissed her with less contemptuous brutality than usual, and he told her that she was a lovely creature and the desire of all men.

He appeared to attach little importance to the

information she vouchsafed, asking her no questions as he paused to light a cigarette.

This forced her to be more explicit, and at last all that she had meant to communicate was exposed.

"You imagine things, my child," he said scoffingly. "I would have to have proof; and then, if it all should be as you say, why, that brooch must be yours, for I know that it is out of real love for me that you talk. And I always pay lavishly for— love."

"Indeed, you know that I adore you, Stépan, and that brooch is just what I want. Stanislass has been niggardly beyond words to me lately, and I am tired of all my other things."

"Bring me some proof at the Reception to-night. I am not dining, but I shall be there by eleven for a few moments."

She agreed, and rose to go, but then she pouted again, and the convex, obstinate curve below her underlip seemed to obtrude itself.

"She has gone back to England, your precious Lady Ardayre, I suppose?"

"She has."

"We shall all meet there in a week or so. Stanislass is going to see some of his boring countrymen in London, the conference you know about, and we have taken a house in Grosvenor Square for some months. I do not know many people yet; will you see to it that I do?"

"I will see that you have as many of these handsome Englishmen as will completely keep your hands full."

She laughed delightedly.

"But it is women I want; the men I can always get for myself."

"Fear nothing, your reception will be great."

Then she flung herself into his arms and embraced him, and then moved towards the door.

"I will telephone to Cartier's in the morning," said Verischenzko as he opened the door for her, "if you bring me some interesting proof of your love for me—tonight."

And when she had gone he took up his letter again and looked at the address:

> To:
>   Lady Ardayre,
>   Ardayre Chase,
>   North Somerset,
>   Angleterre

"I must keep to the things of the spirit with you, precious lady. And when I cannot subdue it, there is Harietta for the flesh. But wough! she sickens me, even for that!"

*   *   *

Denzil Ardayre could not get any more leave for a considerable time and remained quartered in the North.

He played cricket and polo to his heart's content, but the head of the family and his charming wife went through the feverish season of 1914 in the townhouse in Brook Street.

Ardayre was too far away for weekend parties, but they had several successful London dinners, and Amaryllis was becoming quite a capable hostess and was much admired in the Social World.

Very fine of instinct and apprehension at all times, she was developing, by contact with intelligent people, for Sir John had taken care that she mixed only with the most select of his friends.

The De la Paule family had been more than

appreciative of her, and had guided her and supervised her visiting-list with care.

A week after they had come up to Brook Street, the Boleskis arrived at the Mount Lennard House, which they had taken in Grosvenor Square, armed with every kind of introduction, and Harietta immediately began to dazzle the Social World.

Verischenzko had been detained in Paris. The events of June 28 at Sarajevo were of deep concern to him, and it was not until the second week in July that he arrived at the Ritz, full of profound preoccupation.

Amaryllis had been to Harietta's dinners and dances, and now in return the Boleskis had been asked down to Ardayre for the three days at the end of the month, when the coming of age of the young Marquis of Bridgeborough would give occasion for great rejoicings, and Amaryllis herself would give a Ball.

"You cannot ask people down to North Somerset in these days just for the pleasure of seeing you, my dear child," Lady de la Paule had said to her nephew's wife.

"Each season it gets worse. One is flattered if one's friends answer an invitation even to dinner, or remain for half-an-hour when it is done.

"Now Bridgeborough's coming of age will make a nice excuse for you to have a party at Ardayre. How many people can you put up? I should think thirty guests and their servants at least, and seven or eight more if you use the agent's house."

So it had been arranged, and John expressed his pleasure that his sweet Amaryllis should show what a hostess she could be.

None but the most interesting people was invited, and the party promised to be the greatest success.

Two or three days before they were to go down, Amaryllis, coming in late in the afternoon, found Verischenzko's card.

"Oh, John," she cried delightedly, "that very thrilling Russian whom we met in Paris has called. You remember, he wrote to me some time ago and said he would let us know when he arrived. Oh, wouldn't it be nice to have him at our party . . . let us telephone him now!"

Verischenzko answered the call himself and expressed himself as enchanted at the thought of seeing her, and yes, with pleasure he would come down to Ardayre for the Ball.

"We shall meet tonight, perhaps, at Carlton House Terrace at the German Embassy," he said, "and then we can settle everything."

Verischenzko seemed to find her very soon. He was not one of those persons who miss things by vagueness.

His yellow-green eyes were blazing when they met hers, and without any words he offered her his arm, foreign-fashion, and drew her out onto the broad terrace to a secluded seat which he had apparently selected beforehand, as there was no hesitancy in his advance towards this goal.

"I feel when I am with you that I am enveloped in some strong essence," Amaryllis said with a satisfied sigh, "as though I were uplifted and awakened. It is very curious, because you have such a wicked face, but you make me feel that I want to be good."

"We have met, of course, in a former life," he replied, "then, probably, I tempted you to break all vows. It was my fault, so in this life you are to tempt me, it may be, but my will has developed—I mean to resist.

"I want to place you as my joy of the spirit this time; something which is pure and beautiful, apart from earthly things."

Into Amaryllis's mind there flashed the thought that if she saw him often, her emotions for him might not keep at that high level! Her eyes perhaps expressed this doubt, for Verischenzko bent nearer.

"Another must fulfil that which must be denied to me. You are too young to remain free from emotion. Hold yourself until the right time comes."

Amaryllis wondered why he should speak as though it were an understood thing that she could feel no emotion for John. She resented this.

"I have my husband," she answered with dignity and a sweetly conventional air.

"You are delicious when you say things like that," Verischenzko said, laughing, "loyal, and English, and proud.

"But listen, child, it is a waste of time to have any dissimulation with me. We finished all those things when we were lovers in our other life. Now we must be frank and learn of each other. Shall it not be so?"

Amaryllis felt a number of things.

"Yes, you are right; we will always speak the truth."

They had to pass along a corridor to reach the staircase, upon the landing of which they had seen Sir John and *Madame* Boleski leaning over the balustrade.

When they got there, the two had moved on out of sight, so Verischenzko, bowing, left Amaryllis with Lady de la Paule.

As he retraced his steps later on, he saw Sir John Ardayre in earnest conversation with Lemon

Bridges, the fashionable, rising surgeon of the day. They stood in an alcove, and Verischenzko's alert intelligence was struck by the expression on John Ardayre's face.

It was so sad and resigned, as that of a brave man who has received a death sentence. And as he passed close to them he heard these words from John:

"It is quite hopeless, then. I feared so. . . ."

He stopped his descent for a moment and looked again, and then a sudden illumination came into his yellow-green eyes, and he went on down the stairs.

'There is tragedy here; how will it affect the Lady of My Soul?' he wondered to himself.

He walked out of the house and into Pall Mall, and there by the Rag met Denzil Ardayre!

"We seem doomed to have unexpected meetings," cried that young man delightedly. "Here I am only up for one night on regimental business, and I run into you!"

They walked on together, and Denzil went into the Ritz with Verischenzko, and they smoked in his sitting-room.

They talked of many things for a long time— of the unrest in Europe and the clouds in the southeast, of Denzil's political aims, of things in general, and at last Verischenzko said:

"I have just left your cousin and his wife at the German Embassy; they have now gone on to a Ball. He makes an indulgent husband. I suppose the affair is going well?"

"Very well between them, I believe. That sickening cad Ferdinand is circulating rumours that they can never have any children, but they are for his own ends. I must arrange to meet them when I come up next time. I hear that the family are enchanted with Amaryllis."

"She is a thing of flesh and blood and flame. I could love her wildly did I not think it unwise."

Denzil glanced sharply at his friend. He had not often known him to hesitate when attracted by a woman.

They smoked silently for a moment, Verischenzko's face fixed and inscrutable and Denzil's debonair English one unusually grave.

"Someone told me that your friend *Madame* Boleski was having a tremendous success in London. I wish I could have got leave. I should like to have seen the whole thing."

"Harietta is enjoying her luck-moment; she is in her zenith. She has baffled me as to where she receives her information from. She is capable of betraying both sides to gain some material and possibly trivial end.

"She is worth studying, if you do come up, for she is unique. Most criminals have some stable point in immorality, but Harietta is troubled by nothing fixed: no law of God or man means anything to her; she is ruled only by her sense of self-preservation. Her career is picturesque."

"Had she ever any children?"

Verischenzko crossed himself.

"Heaven forbid! Think of watching Harietta's instincts coming out in a child! Poor Stanislass is at least saved that!"

"What a terrible thought that would be to one. But no man thinks of such things in selecting a wife!"

"You will not marry yet—no?"

"Certainly not! There is no necessity that I should. Marriage is only an obligation for the heads of families, not for the younger branches."

"But if Sir John Ardayre has no son, you are —in blood—the next direct heir."

"And Ferdinand is the next direct heir in law. That makes one sick."

Verischenzko poured his friend out a whisky and soda and said, smiling:

"Then let us drink once more to the Ardayre son!"

Chapter
Three

Lady de la Paule really felt proud of her niece, the party at Ardayre was progressing so perfectly.

The guests had all arrived in time for the Ball at Bridgeborough Castle on July 23.

The next day there had been the garden-party, and then a large dinner at Ardayre; and now, on the last night of their stay, Amaryllis's own Ball was to take place.

All the other big country houses round were filled also, and nothing could have been gayer or more splendidly done than the whole thing.

John Ardayre had been quite enthusiastic about all the arrangements, taking the greatest pride in settling everything which could add lustre to his Amaryllis's success as a hostess.

Verischenzko had only just arrived for the Ball and Amaryllis took him across to the other side of the lake.

"I have brought you here," she said, "so that you may get the best view of the house. Indeed, I think it is very beautiful from over the water; do you not?"

Verischenzko remained silent for a moment.

His face had altered in this last week. It looked haggard and thinner, and his peculiar eyes had an intense look about them, as though he was concentrating on something very important.

He took in the perfect picture of this stately English home, with its Henry VII centre and watchtowers and gabled main buildings, and the Queen Anne-style added square, all mellowed and amalgamated into a whole of exquisite beauty and dignity in the glow of the setting sun.

"How proud you should be of such possessions, you English. The accumulation of centuries, conserved by freedom from strike. It is no wonder you are so arrogant!"

He paused, then went on slowly:

"You could not be if you had only memories, as we have, of wooden barracks up to a hundred and fifty years ago, and drunkenness and orgies, and beating of serfs. This is the picture our country houses call up—any of the older ones which have escaped being burnt.

"But here you have traditions of harmony and justice and of obligations to the people nobly fulfilled."

Then he took off his hat and looked up into the golden sky.

"May nothing happen to hurt England, and may we one day be as free."

A shiver ran through Amaryllis, but something kept her silent. She divined that her friend's mood did not desire speech from her yet.

He spoke again, and earnestly, a moment or two afterwards:

"Lady of My Soul, I am going away tomorrow into a frenzied turmoil. I have had news from my country, and I must be in the centre of events. We do not know what will come of it all! I came down today at great sacrifice of time to bid you farewell.

"It may be that I shall never see you again, though I think that I shall; but, should I not, promise me that you will remain my star, unsmirched by the paltriness of the world.

"Promise me that you will live up to the ideal of this noble home, that you will develop your brain and your intuition, and that you will be forceful and filled with common sense.

"I would like to have moulded your spiritual being, and brought you to the highest, but it is not for me, perhaps, in this life; but another will come. See that you live worthily."

Amaryllis was deeply moved.

"Indeed I will try. I have seen so little of you, but I feel that I have known you always, and yes, even I feel that it is true, what you said. . . ."

She grew rosy with confusion.

"That we were . . . lovers. I am so ignorant and undeveloped, not advanced like you, but when you speak you seem to awaken memories."

She paused before she went on:

"It is as though a transitory light gleams in dark places, and I receive flashes of understanding, and then it grows obscured again; but I will try to seize and hold it . . . indeed, I will try to do as you would wish."

They both looked straight ahead at the splendid house, and then Amaryllis looked at Verischenzko, and it seemed as though his face was transfigured with some inward light.

"Strange things are coming, child. The cauldron has boiled over, and we do not know what the stream may engulf. Think of this evening in the days which will be, and remember my words."

His voice vibrated; he did not look at her, but always across the lake, at the house.

"Whenever you are in doubt as to the wisdom of a decision between two courses, put them to the test of which, if you follow it, will enable you to respect your own soul. Never do that which the inward You despises."

"And if both courses look equally good and it is merely a question of earthly benefit?"

"Never be vague." Verischenzko smiled. "There is an Arab proverb which says: 'Trust in God, but tie up your camel.' "

The setting sun was throwing its last gleams upon the windows of the high tower. Nothing more beautiful or impressive than this scene could have been imagined.

Verischenzko gazed at the wonder of it, and his yellow-green eyes were wide with the vision it created in his brain.

No, this should never go to the bastard Ferdinand, whose life in Constantinople was a disgrace. This record of fine living and achievement of worthy Ardayres should remain the glory of the true Ardayre blood.

He turned and looked at Amaryllis sitting at his side, so slender, and strong, and young, and he said:

"It is necessary above all things that you cultivate a steadiness and a clearness of judgement, which will enable you to see the great aim in a thing, and not be hampered by sentimental jingo and convention, which is a danger when a nature is as good and as true, but as undeveloped, as yours.

"Whatever circumstance should arise in your life, in relation to the trust you hold for this family and this home, bring the keenest common sense to bear upon the matter, and keep in view the end, that you must uphold it and pass it on resplendent."

Amaryllis felt that he was transmitting some message to her. His eyes were full of inspiration and seemed to see into the beyond.

What message? She refrained from asking. If he had meant her to understand more fully, he would have told her plainly. Light would come in its own time.

"I promise," was all she said.

They looked at the great tower. The sun had left some of the windows, and in one they could see the figure of a woman standing in some light dressing-gown.

"That is Harietta Boleski," Verischenzko remarked, his mood changing, and that penetrating, inscrutable expression growing in his regard. "It is almost too far away to be certain, but I am sure that it is she. Am I right? Is that window in her room?"

"Yes. How wonderful of you to be able to recognise her at that distance!"

"Of what is she thinking—if one can call her planning 'thoughts'! She does not gaze at views to appreciate the loveliness of the landscape. Figures in the scene are all which could hold her attention, and those figures are you and I."

"Why should we interest her?"

"There are one or two reasons why we should. I think after all you must be very careful of her. I believe if she stays on in England you had better not let the acquaintance increase."

"Very well."

Amaryllis again did not question him; she felt that he knew best.

"She has been most successful here, and at the Bridgeborough Ball she amused herself with a German officer, and left the other women's men alone.

He was brought by the party from Broomsgrove and was most *empressé*," said Amaryllis. Then she continued:

"He got introduced to her at once, just after we came in. I expect they will bring him tonight. He and she looked such a magnificent pair, dancing a quadrille. It was quite a serious Ball to begin with!"

"He was a fine animal, then?" said Verischenzko.

"Yes, but . . . ?"

"You said a *pair*. Only an animal could make a pair with Harietta! Describe him to me. What was he like? And what uniform did he wear?"

Amaryllis gave a description of height and complexion, and of the blue and gold coat he'd worn.

"He would have been really good-looking, except that to our eyes his hips are too wide."

"It sounds typically German; there are hundreds such there, some ordinary Prussian infantry regiment, I expect. You say he was *introduced* to Harietta? They were not old friends?"

"I heard him ask Mrs Nordenheimer, his hostess, who she was, in his guttural voice, and Mrs Nordenheimer came up to me and presented him and asked me to introduce him to my guest. So I did."

"And how did Harietta welcome this partner?"

"She looked a little bored, but afterwards they danced several times together."

"Ah!" And that was all Verischenzko said, but his thoughts ran:

'An infantry officer, not a large enough capture for Harietta to waste time on in a public place, when she is here to advance herself. She danced with him because she was *obliged* to. I must ascertain who this man is.'

Amaryllis saw that he was preoccupied, so she led the way as they walked on now round through the shrubbery on the left, and so at last to the house again. Amaryllis could not chance being late.

*   *   *

Harietta Boleski stamped across her charming, chintz-decorated chamber in the great tower. She was like an angry wolf in the Zoo: she burnt with rage.

Verischenzko had never walked by lakes with her, nor bent over her with that air of devotion!

"He loves that hateful bit of bread and butter! But I shall crush her yet, and Ferdinand Ardayre will help me!" she vowed.

Then she rang her bell violently for Marie, her maid, while she kicked aside Fou-Chou, her Pekinese, who had travelled to England as an adjunct to her beauty, concealed in a cloak.

His minute body quivered with pain and fear, and he looked up at her reproachfully with his round Chinese idol's eyes; then he hid under a chair, where presently Marie found him trembling, and carried him surreptitiously to her room.

"My angel," she told him as they went along the passage, "that she-devil will kill you one day, unless, happily, I can place you in safety first. But if she does, then I will murder her myself! What has caused her fury tonight? Someone has spoilt her game."

*   *   *

In the oak-panelled smoking-room, deserted by all but these two, Verischenzko spoke to Stanislass, hastily and in his own tongue.

"The news is of vital importance, Stanislass. You must return with me to London; of all things, you must show energy now and hold your men together. I leave in the morning.

"You hesitate? Impossible! Harietta keeps you! Bah! Then I will wash my hands of you and of Poland.

"Weakling! To let a woman rule you! Well, if you choose that, you can go by yourself to hell. I have done with you."

Then he strode from the room, looking more savage than ever in his just wrath. And when he had gone, the second husband of Harietta leant forward and buried his head in his hands.

*   *   *

The picture gallery made a brilliant setting for that gallant company. A collection of England's best, dancing their hardest to a stirring band, which sang when the tune of some popular revue chorus came in.

' "The Song of the Swan," ' Verischenzko thought as he observed it all in the last few minutes before midnight.

He must go away soon, he knew.

A messenger had arrived in hot haste from London, motoring beyond the speed-limit, and as soon as his servant had packed his things, he must return and not wait for the morning.

All relations between Austria and Servia had been broken off, the conflagration had begun, and no further time must be wasted. He must be in Russia as soon as it was possible to get there.

He blamed himself for coming down.

'And yet it was as well,' he reflected, because he had become awakened in regard to possible double-dealing from Harietta.

But now where were his host and hostess? He must bid them farewell!

John Ardayre was valsing with Lady Avonwier, and Harietta Boleski undulated in the arms of the tall German who had come with the party from Broomsgrove, but Amaryllis for the moment was absent from the room.

'If I could only know who the beast is before I go, and where she has met him previously.' Verischenzko's thoughts ran. 'It is more than ever necessary that I master her, and there is so little time.'

He waited for a few seconds; the dance was almost done, and when the last notes of music ceased and the throng of people swept towards him, he fixed Harietta with his eye.

Her evening so far had not been agreeable. She had not been able to have a word with Stépan, who had been far from her at the banquet before the Ball.

She was torn with jealousy of Amaryllis; and the advent of Hans, when she had wished to be free to regrab Verischenzko, had been most unfortunate.

It had not been altogether pleasant, his turning up at Bridgeborough, but at any rate that one evening was quite enough! She really could not be wearied with him more!

His new instructions to her from the Higher Command were more annoyingly difficult too, coming at a time when her whole mind was given to consolidating her position in England.

It was really too bad!

If only the tiresome bothers of these stupid old quarrelling countries did not upset matters, she just meant to make Stanislass shut up his ugly old Polish home and settle in some splendid country house like this, only nearer London.

Now that she had seen what life was like in England, she knew that this was her goal.

No bothersome old other language to be learned; besides, no other men were as good-looking as the English, or made such safe and prudent lovers, because they did not boast.

If any information she had been able to collect for Hans in the last year had helped his Over-Lords to stir up trouble, she was almost sorry she had given it.

Unless, of course, ructions between those ridiculous southern countries made it so that she could remain in England; then it was a good thing.

And Hans had assured her that England could not be dragged in. Then she laughed to herself as she always did when Hans coerced her when she recollected how she had given his secrets away to Verischenzko, and that no matter how he seemed to compel her obedience, she was even with him underneath!

She looked now at the Russian standing there, so tall and ugly and yet weirdly distinguished, and a wild, passionate desire for him overcame her, as primitive as that which a savage might have felt.

At that moment she almost hated her first husband, for she dared not wait until Verischenzko spoke to her. Hans could not prevent that, nor could he accuse her of disobeying his command.

So it was with joy that she saw the Russian approach her. She did not know that he was leaving suddenly, and she was wondering if some meeting could be arranged for later on, when Hans would be gone.

"Good-evening, *Madame!*" Verischenzko said suavely. "May I not have the pleasure of a turn with you? It is delightful to meet you again."

Harietta slipped her hand out of Hans's arm, and stood still, determined to secure Stépan at once, since the chance had come.

Verischenzko divined her intention, and continued, his voice serious with its mock respect:

"I wonder if I could persuade you to come with me and find your husband. You know the house and I do not. I have something I want to talk to him about, if you won't think me a great bore, taking you from your partner. . . ."

He bowed politely to Hans.

Harietta introduced them casually, and then said archly:

"I am sure you will excuse me, Captain von Pickelheim; and don't forget you have the first one-step after supper!"

So Hans was dismissed with a ravishing smile.

Verischenzko had watched the German covertly, and he saw that, with all his forced stolidity, an angry gleam had come into his eyes.

'They have certainly met before; and he knows me. I must somehow make time.'

Then aloud he said:

"You are looking a dream of beauty tonight, Harietta. Is there not some quiet corner in the garden where we can be alone for a few minutes? You drive me mad."

Harietta loved to hear this, and in triumph she raised her head and drew him into one of the sitting-rooms, and so out through the open windows and on into the darkness beyond the illuminations of the lawn.

Twenty minutes afterwards, Verischenzko entered the house alone, a grim smile of satisfaction upon his rugged countenance.

Jealousy, acting on animal passion, had been for once as productive of information as a ruby ring or brooch—and what a remarkable type, Harietta! Could there be anything more elemental on the earth?

Meanwhile, this lady had gained the Ballroom by another door, delighted with her adventure and the thought that she had tricked Hans!

"Have you seen our hostess, *Madame?*" the Russian asked, meeting Lady de la Paule. "I have been looking for her everywhere. Is not this a charming sight?"

They stayed and talked for a few minutes, watching the joyous company of dancers, among whom Amaryllis could now be seen.

Verischenzko wished to say farewell to her when the one-step should be done. They would all be going in to supper, and then would be his chance. He could not delay longer. He must be gone.

He was paying bare attention to what Lady de la Paule was saying. Her fat voice prattled on:

"I hope these tiresome little quarrels of the Balkan peoples will settle themselves. If Austria should go to war with Servia, it may upset my Carlsbad cure."

Then he laughed out suddenly, but instantly checked himself.

"That would be too unfortunate, *Madame.* We must not anticipate such preposterous happenings!"

And as he walked forward to meet Amaryllis his face was set; and he thought:

'Half the civilised world thinks thus of things.

The sinister events in the Balkans convey no suggestions of danger, and only matter in that they could upset a Carlsbad cure! Alas, how sound asleep these splendid people are!'

He met Amaryllis and briefly told her that he must go. She left her partner and came with him to the foot of the staircase which led to his room.

"Good-bye, and God keep you," she said feelingly, but she noticed that he did not even offer to take her hand.

"All blessings, my star," he said, and his voice was hoarse; then he turned abruptly and went on up the stairs.

But when he reached the landing above, he paused and looked down at her, moving away among the throng.

"Sweet Lady of My Soul," he whispered softly. "After Harietta, I could not soil even your glove!"

* * *

Events moved rapidly. Of what use to write of those restless, feverish days before August 4, 1914? They are too well known to all the world.

John, as ever, did his duty, and at once put his name down for active service, and trained with the North Somerset Yeomanry, in anticipation of being soon sent to France.

But before all this happened, the night war was declared he remained in his own sitting-room at Ardayre, and Amaryllis wondered, and towards dawn crept out of bed and listened in the passage, but no sound came from within the room.

How very unsatisfactory this strange reserve between them was becoming. Would she never be able to surmount it? Must they go to the end of their lives, living like two polite, friendly acquaintances, neither sharing the other's thoughts?

She hardly realised that the war could personally concern John.

The Yeomanry, she imagined, were only for home defence, so at this stage no anxiety troubled her about her husband.

The next day he seemed frightfully preoccupied, and then he talked to her seriously of their home and its traditions, and how she must love it and understand its meaning.

He spoke too of his great wish for a child, and Amaryllis wondered at the tone almost of anguish in his voice.

"If only we had a son, Amaryllis, I would not care what came to me; a true Ardayre to carry on! The thought of Ferdinand here after me drives me perfectly mad!"

Amaryllis did not know what to answer. She looked down and clasped her hands.

John came close and gazed into her face, as if some comfort could be found, then he folded her in his arms.

"Oh, Amaryllis!" he said, and sighed.

"What is it? Oh, what does everything mean?" she cried. "Why, why can't we have a son like other people of our age?"

John kissed her again.

"It shall be—it must be so," he answered, and framed her face in his hands.

"Amaryllis, I know you have often wondered whether I really love you. You have found me a stupid, unsatisfactory sort of husband; indeed, I am but a dull companion at the best of times.

"Well, I want you to know that I do, and I am going to try to change, dear little girl. If I knew that I held some corner of your heart, it would comfort me."

"Of course you do, John. Alas, if you would only unbend and be loving to me, how happy we could be!"

"I will try." And he kissed her once more.

That afternoon he went up to London to his medical board, and Amaryllis was to join him in Brook Street on the following day.

She was stunned like everyone else. War seemed a nightmare, an unreality; she had not grasped its meaning as yet.

That evening when John Ardayre arrived he paced up and down in the library for half-an-hour; he was very pale, and lines of thought were stamped upon his brow.

He had come to a decision: there only remained the details of a course of action to be arranged.

He went to the telephone and called up the Cavalry Club.

Yes, Captain Ardayre was in; and presently Denzil's voice said in surprise:

"Hullo!"

"I heard by chance that you were in town. I suppose your regiment will be going out at once. It is your cousin, John Ardayre, speaking; we have not met since you were a boy. I have something rather vital I want to say to you. Could you possibly come round?"

The two voices were so alike in tone it was quite remarkable; each was aware of it as he listened to the other.

"Where are you, and what is the time?"

"I am in our house in Brook Street, number one hundred two, and it is nearly seven. Could you manage to come now?"

There was a pause of a second or two, then Denzil said:

"All right, I will get into a taxi and be with you in about five minutes."

John Ardayre grew paler still and sank into a chair.

His hands were trembling; this sign of weakness angered him, and he got up and rang the bell, and ordered his valet, who had come up with him, to bring him some brandy.

Murcheson was an old and valued servant, and he looked at his master with concern, but he knew him too well to make any remark.

If there was anyone in the world, beyond the great surgeon Lemon Bridges, who could understand the preoccupations of John Ardayre, Murcheson was the man.

He brought the cognac immediately, and retired from the room a moment or two before Denzil arrived.

Very little trace of emotion remained upon the face of the head of the family when his cousin was shown in, and he came forward cordially to meet him.

Standing opposite each other, they might have been brothers, not cousins, the resemblance was so strong!

Denzil was perhaps fairer, but their heads were both small, and their limbs had the same long lines. But whereas John Ardayre suggested undemonstrative stolidity, every atom of the younger man was live vitality.

His eyes were bluer, his hair was more bronze, and exuberant perfect health glowed in his tanned fresh skin.

Both their voices were peculiarly deep, with the pronunciation of the words especially refined.

John Ardayre said some civil things with composure, and Denzil replied in kind, explaining how he had been most anxious to meet John and Amaryllis and heal the breach the fathers had made.

John offered him a cigar, and finally the atmosphere seemed to be unfrozen as they smoked. But in Denzil's mind there was speculation. It was not for just this that he had been asked to come round.

John began to speak presently, with a note of deep seriousness in his voice.

He talked of the war and of his Yeomanry's going out, and of Denzil's regiment also. It was quite on the cards that they might both be killed.

Then he spoke of Ferdinand, and the old story of the shame, and he told Denzil of his boyhood and its great trials, and of his determination to redeem the family home.

He went on to tell of the great luck which had befallen him in the city after the South African War, and how the thought of worthily handing on the inheritance in the direct male line had become the dominating desire of his life.

At first his manner had been very restrained, but gradually the intense feeling which was vibrating in him made itself known, and Denzil grew to realise how profound was his love for Ardayre, and how great his family pride.

But underneath all this some absolute agony must be wringing his soul.

Denzil became increasingly interested.

At last John seemed to have come to a very difficult part of his narration: he got up from his chair and walked rapidly up and down the room, then forced himself to sit down again and resume his original calm.

"I am going to trust you, Denzil, with something which matters far more than my life."

John looked at Denzil straight in the eyes.

"And I will confide in you because you are next in the direct line. Listen very carefully, please; it concerns your honour in the family as well as mine.

"It would be too infamous to let Ardayre go to the bastard Ferdinand, the snake-charmer's son, if, as is quite possible, I shall be killed in the coming time."

Denzil felt some strange excitement permeating him. What did these words portend?

Beads of perspiration appeared on John's forehead, and his voice sank so low that his cousin bent forward to be certain of hearing him.

Then John spoke in broken sentences, for the first time in his life letting another share the thoughts which tortured him.

Now was not the time for reticence. Denzil must understand everything, so that he would consent to a certain plan.

At length, all that was in John's heart had been made plain, and, exhausted with the effort of his innermost being's unburdenment, he sank back in his chair, deadly pale.

The quiet, waiting attitude in Denzil had given way to keenness, and more than once as he listened to the moving narration he had emitted words of sympathy and concern.

But when the actual plan which John had evolved was unfolded to him, and the part he was to play explained, he rose from his chair and stood leaning on the high mantelpiece.

There was an expression of excitement and illumination on his strong, good-looking face.

"Do not say anything for a little," John said. "Think over everything quietly.

"I am not asking you to do anything dishonourable; and however much I had hated his mother, I would not ask this of you if Ferdinand were my father's son."

He shivered.

"You are the next real heir. Ferdinand could not be: my father had never met the woman until a month before he married her, and the baby arrived five months afterwards, at its full time.

"There was no question of incubators or difficulties and special precautions to rear him, nor was there any suggestion that he was a seven-months child.

"It was only in after years that I found out when my father first saw the woman; but even before that proof, there were many and convincing evidences that Ferdinand was no Ardayre."

"One has only to look at the beast!" cried Denzil. "If the mother was a Bulgarian, he's a mongrel Turk; there is not a trace of English blood in his body!"

"Then surely you agree with me that it would be an infamy if he should take the place of the head of the family, should I not survive?"

Denzil clenched his hands.

"There is no moral question attached, remember," John went on anxiously before his cousin could reply. "There is only the question of the law, which has been tricked and defamed by my father, for the meanest ends of revenge towards me."

He paused to say slowly:

"Now we, you and I, have the right to save the family and its honour and circumvent the perfidy and weakness of that one man."

He waited.

"Oh, can't you understand what this means to me, since for this trust of Ardayre, which I feel I must faithfully carry on, I am willing to ...! Oh, my God, I can't say it!

"Denzil, answer me, tell me that you look at it in the same way as I do. You are of the family.

"It is your blood which Ferdinand would depose; the disgrace would be yours then, since if Ferdinand reigned I would have gone."

The two men were standing opposite each other, and both their faces were pale and stern, but Denzil's blue eyes were blazing with some wonderful new emotion as they looked at John.

"Very well," he said, and held out his hand.

"I appreciate the tremendous faith you have placed in me, and on my word of honour as an Ardayre, I will not abuse it, nor take advantage of it afterwards.

"My regiment will go out at once, I suppose; the chances are as likely that I shall be killed as you."

They shook hands silently.

"We must lose no time."

Then John poured out two glasses of brandy, and the toast they drank was unspoken. But suddenly Denzil remembered as a strange coincidence that he was drinking this toast for the third time.

*   *   *

Amaryllis arrived from Ardayre the next afternoon.

After John's medical board had been squared into pronouncing him fit for active service, he met his wife at the station and was particularly solicitous of her well-being.

He seemed to be unusually glad to see her,

and put his arm round her in the motor, driving to Brook Street.

What would she like to do? They could not, of course, go to the theatre, but if she would rather, they could go out to a restaurant to dine; there were going to be all kinds of difficulties about food.

Amaryllis, who responded immediately to the smallest advance on his part, glowed now with fond sweetness.

She had been so miserable without him, so crushed and upset by the thought of war and his possible participation in it.

All the long night, alone at Ardayre, she had tried to realise what it all would mean. It was too stupendous, she could not grasp it as yet, it was just a blank horror.

But now, to be in the motor and close to him, with everything ordinary and as usual, seemed to drive the hideous fact further and further away. She would not face it for tonight; she would try to be happy and banish the remembrance.

No one knew what was happening, nor if the Expeditionary Force had or had not crossed to France.

John asked her again what she would like to do.

She did not want to go out at all, she told him.

If the kitchen-maid and Murcheson could find them something to eat, she would much rather dine alone with him, and afterwards she would play nice things for him, and John agreed.

When she came down ready for dinner, she was radiant; she had put on a new and ravishing tea-gown, and her grey eyes were shining with a winsome challenge, and her beautiful skin was brilliant with health and freshness.

A man could not have desired a more delectable creature to call his own.

John thought so, and at dinner expanded and told her so.

He was not a practised lover; women had played a very small part in his life, always too filled with work and the one dominating idea to make room for them.

He had none of the tender graciousness ready at his command which Denzil would very well have known how to show. But he loved Amaryllis, and this was the first time he had permitted the expression of his emotion to appear.

She became ever more fascinating, and at length unconscious passion grew in her glance.

John said some rather clumsy but loving things, and when they went back to the library he slipped his arm round her and drew her to his side.

"I love to be near you, John," she whispered. "I like your being so tall and so distinguished-looking, and I like your clothes, they are so well made."

Then she wrinkled her pretty nose.

"And I adore the smell of what you put on your hair! Oh, I don't know, I just want to be in your arms!"

John kissed her.

"I must give you a bottle of that lotion; it is supposed to do wonders for the hair.

"It was originally made by an old housekeeper of my mother's family in the still-room, and I have always kept the recipe. There are cloves in it and some other aromatic herbs."

"Yes, that is what I smell, like a clove carnation. It is divine!

"I wonder why scents have such an effect upon one, don't you? Perhaps I am a very sensuous creature. They can make me feel wicked or good.

"Some scents make me deliciously intoxicated. That one of yours does. When I get near you I want you to hold me and kiss me, John."

Every fibre of John Ardayre's being quivered with pain. The cruel, ironical bitterness of things.

"I've never smelt this same scent on anyone else," she went on, rubbing her soft cheeks up and down against his shoulder in the most alluring way. "I should know it anywhere, for it means just my dear John!"

He turned away, on the pretence of getting a cigarette. He knew that his eyes had filled with tears.

Then Murcheson came into the room with the coffee, and this made a break, and he immediately asked her to play to him, and settled himself in one of the big chairs.

He was too much on the rack to continue any more love-making; the "what might have been" caused too poignant anguish.

He watched her delicate profile outlined against the curtain of green silk. She was so pure and young, and her long throat was white as milk.

If by this time next year she should have a child, a son, and if he himself had not been killed but was sitting there, perhaps watching her holding it—how would he feel then?

Would the certainty of having an Ardayre to carry on heal the wild rebellion in his soul?

'O God,' he prayed silently, 'take away all feeling, and reward this sacrifice by letting the family go on.'

"You don't think you will really have to go to the war, do you, John?" Amaryllis asked after she left the piano. "It will be all over, won't it, before the New Year? And in any case the Yeomanry are only for home defence, aren't they?"

She took a low seat and rested her head against his arm.

John stroked her hair.

"I am afraid it will not be over for a long time, Amaryllis. Yes, I think we shall go out, and pretty soon. You would not wish to stop me, would you, child?"

Amaryllis looked straight in front of her.

"What is this thing in us, John, which makes us feel that, yes, we would give our nearest and dearest, even if they must be killed?

"When the big thing comes even into lives which have been perhaps all frivolous like mine, it seems to make a great light. There is an exultation, and a pity, and a glory, and a grief, but no holding back. It is patriotism, John?"

"That is one name for it, darling."

"But it is really beyond that in this war, because we are going to fight not for England but for right.

"I think that feeling, that we must give, is some oblation of the soul which has freed itself from the chains of the body at last. And for so many years we have all been asleep."

"This is a rude awakening."

They were silent for a little while, each busy with unusual thoughts.

There was a sense of nearness between them, of understanding, new and dangerously sweet.

Amaryllis felt it deliciously, sensuously, and took joy in the fact that she was touching him.

John thrust the feeling away.

'I must get through tonight,' he thought, 'but I cannot if this hideous pain of knowledge of what I must renounce conquers me. I must be strong.'

He went on stroking her hair. It made her

thrill, and she turned and bit one of his fingers playfully, with a wicked little laugh.

"I wish I knew what I am feeling, John," she whispered, and her eyes were aflame. "I wish I knew. . . ."

"I must teach you!" And with sudden fierceness he bent down and kissed her lips.

Then he told her to go to bed.

"You must be tired, Amaryllis, after your journey. Go, like a good child."

She pouted. She was vibrating with some totally new and overmastering emotion. She wanted to stay and be made love to.

She wanted she knew not what, only everything in her was thrilling with passionate warmth.

"Must I? It is only ten."

"I have a frightful lot of business things to write tonight, Amaryllis. Go now and sleep, and I will come and wake you about twelve!"

"Ah! If you would only come now!" she said with a sigh.

He kissed her almost roughly again and led her to the door, and he stood watching her with burning eyes as she went up the stairs.

Then he came back and rang the bell.

"I shall be very late, Murcheson; do not sit up. I will turn out the lights. Good-night."

"Very good, Sir John."

And the valet left the room.

But John Ardayre did not write any business letters; he sank back into his great leather chair, his lips were trembling, and presently sobs shook him, and he leaned forward and buried his face in his hands.

Just before twelve had struck, he went out into the hall and turned off the light at the main. The whole house would now be in absolute darkness—but for an electric torch he carried.

He listened; there was not a sound.

Then he crept quietly up to his dressing-room and returned with a bottle of the clove-scented hair-lotion.

'What a mercy she spoke of it,' his thoughts ran. 'How sensitive women are. I should never have remembered such a thing.'

Yes ... now there was a sound.

*   *   *

Midnight had struck, and Amaryllis, sleeping peacefully, had been dreaming of John.

"Oh, dearest," she whispered drowsily, as, but half-awakened, she felt herself being drawn into a pair of strong arms.

"Oh, you know I love that scent of cloves. Oh ... I love you, John!"

Chapter
Four

When Amaryllis awoke in the morning, her head rested on John's breast and his arm encircled her.

She raised herself on her elbow and looked at him. He was still asleep, and his face was infinitely sad.

She bent over and kissed him with shy tenderness, but he did not move, he only sighed heavily as he lay there.

Why should he look so sad, when they were so happy?

She thought of the loving things he had said to her at dinner, and then afterwards! And she thrilled with emotion.

Life seemed a glorious thing, and . . .

But John was sad, of course, because he must go away.

The recollection of this fact came upon her suddenly like a blast of cold air.

They must part!

War hung there with its hideous shadow, and John must have been conscious of it even in his dreams; that was why he sighed.

The irony of things . . . now . . . when . . .

Oh, how cruel that he must go!

Then John awoke with a shudder, and saw her there, leaning over him with a new, soft love-light in her eyes, and he realised that the anguish of his calvary had only just begun.

She was perfectly exquisite at breakfast. A fresh and tender graciousness radiated in her every glance, and she was subtle and captivating, teasing him that he had been so silent in the night.

"Why wouldn't you talk to me, John? But it was all divine. I did not mind."

Then she became full of winsome ways and caresses, which she had hitherto been too timid to express; and every fond word she spoke stabbed John's heart.

Could she not come and stay somewhere near, so as to be with him while he was in training? It was unbearable to remain alone.

But he told that this would be impossible and that she must go back to Ardayre.

"I will get leave, if there is a chance, my darling."

"Oh, John, you must!"

After he had gone out to the War Office, she sang as she undid a bundle of late roses he had sent her from Soloman's on his way.

She must put them in water herself; no servant should have this pleasing task.

Was it the thought of the imminence of separation which had altered John into so dear a lover?

She went over his words there in the library. And she relived the joy of his sudden fierce kiss, when he had said that he must teach her what her emotions meant.

Ah, how good to learn! How all-glorious was life and love!

"Sweetheart!" The word rang in her ears. He had never called her that before! Indeed, John rarely ever used any term of endearment, and never had got beyond "dear" or "darling" before.

But now it was an exquisite remembrance!

Just the murmured word "sweetheart," whispered softly again and again in the night.

John came back to lunch, but two of the De la Paule family also dropped in, and the talk was of war and the difficulty of getting money at the banks, and how food would become scarce, and what the whole thing would mean.

But over Amaryllis some spell had fallen; nothing seemed a reality, she could not attend to ordinary things, and she felt that she moved and spoke as one still in a dream.

The world, and life, and death, and love were all a blended mystery which was but beginning to unravel for her and draw her nearer to John.

The days went on apace.

John, in camp, thanked God for the strenuous work of his training, that it kept him so occupied that he had barely time to think of Amaryllis or the tragedy of things.

When he had left her on the following afternoon, August 7, she had returned to Ardayre alone, where she began the knitting and shirt-making and amateurish hospital committees which all well-meaning Englishwomen vaguely grasped at before the stern necessities brought them organised work to do.

Amaryllis wrote constantly to John all through August, and many of the letters contained loving allusions which made him wince with pain.

Then came the awful news of Mons, then the Marne and the Aisne, awful and glorious, and a hush and mourning fell over the land; and Amaryllis, like everyone else, lost interest in all personal things for a time.

A young cousin had been killed, and many of her season's partners and friends, and now she knew that the North Somerset Yeomanry would shortly go out and fight, as they had volunteered at once.

She was very miserable.

But when September came, in spite of all this general sorrow, a new horizon presented itself, lit up as if by approaching dawn; for a hope had gradually developed, a hope which would mean the rejoicing of John's heart.

And when first this possibility of future fulfillment was pronounced a certainty, the way was one of almost exalted happiness.

After Dr Geddis drove away down the Northern Avenue, Amaryllis seized a coat from the folded pile of John's in the hall and walked out into the park hatless, the wind blowing the curly tendrils of her soft brown hair, a radiance not of earth in her eyes.

The late September sun was sinking, and gilding the windows of the noble house, and she turned and looked back at it when she was far across the lake.

And the whole of her spirit rose in thankfulness to God, while her soul sang a glad Magnificat.

She too might hand on this great and splendid inheritance! She too would be the mother of Ardayres!

And now to write to John! That was a fresh pleasure!

What would he say? What would he feel? Dear John!

His letters had been calm and matter-of-fact, but that was his way. She did not mind it now.

He loved her, and what did words matter now, with this glorious knowledge in her heart.

To have a baby! Her very own, and John's.

How wonderful! How utterly divine!

Her little feet hardly touched the moss beneath them, she wanted to skip and sing.

Next May! Next May!

A spring flower, a little life to care for, when the war of course would have ended and all the world again could be happy and young!

And then she returned to the tiny ancient church. She had the key to it, a golden one which John had given her on their first visit there. It hung on her bracelet with her own private key.

The sun was pouring through the western window, carpeting the altar steps in translucent cloth of gold.

Amaryllis stole up the short aisle, and paused when she came between the two tall canopied tombs of recumbent sixteenth-century knights, which made so dignified a screen for the little side-aisles; and then she moved on and knelt in the shaft of the sunlight there at the curved rails.

And no one ever raised to God a purer or more fervent prayer.

She stayed until the sun sank below the window, and then she rose and went back to the house, and up to her cedar room.

Now she must write to John!

She began once, twice, but tore up each sheet. Her news was a supreme happiness, but so difficult to transmit!

At last she finished three sides of her own rather large-sized note-paper, but as she read over what she had written, she was not quite content.

It did not express all that she desired John to know.

But how could a mere letter convey the wordless gladness in her heart?

She wanted to tell him how she would worship their baby, and how she would pray that they should be given a son, and how she would remember all his love-words spoken that last time they were together, and weave the joy of them round the little form, so that it should grow strong and beautiful and radiant, and come to earth welcomed and blessed!

Something of all this finally did get written, and she concluded with: `

> *John, is it not all wonderful and blissful and mysterious, this coming proof of our love?*
> *And when I lie awake I say over and over again the sweet name you called me, and which I want to sign! I am not just Amaryllis any longer, but your very own*
> *Sweetheart!*

John received this letter in camp by the afternoon post. He sat down alone in his tent and read and reread each line. Then he stiffened and remained icily still.

He could not analyse his emotions. They were so intermixed with thankfulness and pain, and underneath there was a fierce, primitive jealousy burning.

"Sweetheart!" he said aloud, as though the word were anathema! "And must I call her that, 'sweetheart'! O God, it is too hard!" And he clenched his hands.

By the same post came a letter from Denzil, of whose movements he had asked to be kept informed, saying that the 110th Hussars were going out at once, so they would probably soon meet in France.

Then John wrote to Amaryllis.

The very force of his feeling seemed to freeze his power of expression, and when he had finished he knew that it was but a cold, lifeless thing he had produced, quite inadequate as an answer to her tender, exalted words.

"My poor little girl," he said with a sigh as he read it. "I know this will disappoint her. What a hideous, sickening mockery everything is."

He forced himself to add a postscript, a practice very foreign to his usual methodical rule.

"Never forget that I love you, Amaryllis sweetheart!"

Then he went to his colonel and asked for two days' leave, and when it was granted for the following Saturday and Sunday, he wired to his wife, asking her to meet him in Brook Street.

"I must see her; I cannot bear it!" he cried to himself.

And late at night he wrote to Denzil; it was just that he should do this.

"My wife is going to have a baby," he stated in the letter. "If only it should be a son, then it will not so much matter if both of us are killed; at least the family will be saved and be able to carry on."

He tried to make the letter cordial, for Denzil had behaved with the most perfect delicacy throughout, he must admit.

And although they had met once and exchanged several letters, not the faintest allusion to the subject of their talk in the library at Brook Street had ever been made by him.

Denzil had indeed acted and written as though such knowledge between them did not exist.

He, Denzil, in these last seven weeks had been extremely occupied.

And while his forces were concentrated upon the exhilarating preparations for war, it would happen in rare moments before sleep claimed him at night that he would let his thoughts conjure a waking dream which was infinitely, mystically sweet.

And every pulse would thrill with ecstasy, and then his will would banish it, and he would think of other subjects.

He could not face the marvel of his emotions at this period, nor dwell upon the romantically exciting aspect of some things.

He was up in London upon equipment business on the very Saturday that John got leave, and he was due to dine at the Carlton with Verischenzko, who had that day arrived on vital matters.

As they came into the hall, a man stopped to talk to the Russian, and Denzil's eye wandered over the numerous and depressed-looking company collected, waiting for their parties to arrive.

Even in those early autumn days war had set its grim seal upon the festive spot. People looked rather ashamed of being seen, and no one smiled.

He nodded to one or two friends, and then his glance fell upon a beautiful, slim, brown-haired girl, sitting quietly waiting in an arm-chair by the restaurant steps.

She wore a plain black frock, but in her belt one huge, crimson clove carnation was unostentatiously tucked.

'What a lovely creature!' his thoughts ran.

And then Verischenzko turned from his acquaintance at that moment, and Denzil said to him as they started to advance:

"Stépan, if you want to see something typically English and perfectly exquisite, look at that girl in the arm-chair opposite where the band used to be. I wonder who she is."

"What luck!" cried Verischenzko. "That is your cousin, Amaryllis Ardayre. Come along."

And in a second Denzil found himself being introduced to her, and being greeted by her with interested cordiality, as befitted their cousinly relationship.

But Verischenzko, whose eyes missed nothing, remarked that under his sunburn Denzil had grown suddenly very pale.

Amaryllis was enchanted to see her friend the Russian.

John had gone to the telephone, it appeared; and yes, they were dining alone, and of course she was sure John would love to amalgamate parties.

It was so nice of Verischenzko to think of it! And there was John now.

The blood rushed back to Denzil's heart and the colour to his face—he had only murmured a few conventional words.

Mercifully, John would decide the matter; it was not Denzil's doing that he and Amaryllis had met.

John caught sight of the three as he came along the balcony from the telephone, so he had time to take in the situation.

He saw that the meeting was quite *imprévu*, and he had of course no choice but to accept Verischenzko's suggestion with a show of grace.

At that very moment, before they could enter the restaurant and rearrange their tables, Harietta Boleski and her husband swept upon them; they were staying in the hotel.

Harietta was enraptured.

What a delightful surprise meeting them! Were they all just together? Would they not dine with her and her husband?

She purred these sentiments to John, while her eyes took in with satisfaction Denzil's extraordinary good looks; and there was Stépan too! Nothing could be more agreeable than to scintillate for them both.

John hailed their arrival with relief; it would relax the intolerable strain which both he and Denzil would be bound to experience.

So, looking at the rest of the party, he indicated that he thought they would accept. It suited Verischenzko also, for his own reasons. And any suggestion to enlarge the intimate number of four would have been received by Denzil with graciousness.

Denzil had not imagined that he would feel such profound emotion on seeing Amaryllis, and the intensity of it caused him displeasure. It was altogether such a remarkable situation.

He knew that it would have been of thrilling interest to him had it not been for the presence of John.

His knowledge of what John must be suffering, and the knowledge that John was aware of what he also must be feeling, turned the whole circumstance into discomfort.

As soon as he recalled himself to *Madame* Boleski, they all went into the restaurant, to the Boleski table, just inside the door, by the window on the right.

Before the end of the dinner, Amaryllis, against her will, was conscious of the fact that Denzil was studiously avoiding any conversation with her beyond what the exigencies of politeness required.

He devoted himself entirely to Harietta, to her delight, and Verischenzko and Amaryllis talked, while John was left to Stanislass.

But the very fact of Denzil's likeness to John made Amaryllis look at him, and she resented his attraction and the interest he aroused in her.

His voice was perhaps even deeper than John's; and how extraordinarily well his bronze-coloured hair was planted on his forehead; and how perfectly groomed and brushed and soldierly he looked!

He had taken the measure of *Madame* Boleski too, and was apparently enjoying with a cultivated subtlety the act of drawing her out.

He was no novice, it seemed; and there was a whimsical light in his eyes, and once or twice they had inadvertently met hers with understanding, when Verischenzko had made some especially cryptic remark.

She knew that she would very much like to talk to him.

Verischenzko was observing her carefully. There was a new expression in her eyes which puzzled him. Her features seemed to be drawn with finer lines, and pale violet shadows lay beneath her grey eyes.

Was it the gloom of the war which oppressed her? It could not be altogether that, because her regard was serene and even happy.

'Did I not know that nothing could be more unlikely, I should say she was going to have a child. What is the mystery?'

He found himself very much interested.

Especially he was anxious to watch what impression Denzil made upon her. He saw, as the dinner went on, that Amaryllis was aware that he was an attractive creature.

'There is the beginning of a chapter of necessary and expedient romance here,' he thought.
'If only Denzil is not killed.'

But what did his growing so pale on learning
that she was his cousin mean . . . ?

That was not a natural reaction; some deep
undercurrents had been stirred. And in what way
was all this going to affect the Lady of His Soul?

They could not have any intimate conversation at dinner; they spoke of ordinary things and
the war and the horror of it. Russia was moving
forward, but Verischenzko did not appear to be
very optimistic in spite of this.

There were things in his country, he told
Amaryllis, which might handicap the fighting.

Stanislass Boleski looked extremely depressed.
He had a hang-dog, strained mien, and Verischenzko's contemptuously friendly attitude towards him wounded him deeply.

Once he had shone as a leader and chief in
Stépan's life; but now, alas, after the stormy scene
in the smoking-room at Ardayre, that he could
greet him casually and not turn from him in anger showed to where he had sunk in Verischenzko's
estimation—a thing of naught, not even worth
his disapproval.

The dinner to him was a painful trial.

John also was far from content. He had been
longing to see Amaryllis, and yet the sight of her
and her fond and insinuating words and caresses
had caused him exquisite suffering.

His emotions were so varied and complex.
His prayer had been answered, but apart from his
natural loathing for all subterfuge, every new tenderness towards himself which Amaryllis dis-
played aroused some indefinable jealousy.

She had been so glad to see him, and he had

been conscious himself that he had been unusually stolid and self-contained towards her.

He knew that she grew disappointed, and that probably the exalted sentiment which her letter had indicated that she was feeling had been chilled before she could put it into words.

All this distressed him, and yet he could not break through the reserve of his nature.

And now, to crown unfortunate things, there was Denzil, brought by fate and no one's manoeuvering into Amaryllis's company!

Of all things, he had hoped that they need not meet before he and his cousin should go to the Front.

And it had all been brought about by his own action in insisting that they dine at a restaurant, as the kitchen-maid who always remained at Brook Street had gone to see a wounded brother.

Amaryllis had sighed a little as she had consented, with the faint protest that they could have eaten something cold.

But on their drive to the Carlton she had become fondly affectionate again, nestling close to him, and then she had pulled out the carnation from her belt and held it for him to smell.

"I picked it in the greenhouse this morning, the last of them; I have had them all round me while there were any, because they remind me of you, dearest . . . and of everything divine."

John felt that he should always now hate that clove lotion for the hair, and he could no longer bear to use it.

He was perfectly aware that Denzil, on his hostess's other side, was looking everything that a woman could desire, and that his easy casualness of manner would be likely to charm.

He saw that Amaryllis too observed him with

unconscious interest, and a feeling akin to despair filled his heart.

Life for him had always been difficult, and he was accustomed to blows, but this one was particularly hard to bear, because he really loved Amaryllis and desired a happiness with her which he knew could never really be attained.

Only Harietta, of the whole party, was quite content. She intended to annex Stépan when they should be drinking coffee in the hall.

She looked upon Denzil's conquest now as almost an accomplished fact, and so felt that she might let him talk to Amaryllis, since the Russian was her real object.

"Why aren't you staying in the hotel, darling brute?" she whispered to him as they left the restaurant. "If you had been . . ."

"I am," said Verischenzko.

And leaving her for a moment, he went and telephoned to his not unintelligent Russian servant at the Ritz, to arrange for the transference of his rooms:

"She requires the most careful watching. I must waste no time."

And then he returned to the party in the hall.

*   *   *

Denzil Ardayre took up his letters, which had been forwarded to him from the depot where he was stationed.

He and Verischenzko were passing through the hall of his mother's house, for a talk and a smoke in his sitting room, after leaving the Carlton.

The house was in St. James's Place, a small, old building, the ground floor of which was given over to Denzil whenever he was in London.

His mother was absent, having gone to Bath, where she spent a long autumn cure.

John's letter lay on the top, and Verischenzko caught the look of interest which came into Denzil's face.

"Don't mind me, my dear chap," he remarked. "Read your letters."

And they went on into the sitting-room.

"I want just to look at this one; it is from John Ardayre, whom we met tonight." Denzil opened it casually. "I wonder what he is writing to me about—he did not say anything at dinner."

He read the short communication and exclaimed:

"Good God!"

Then he checked himself.

He was obviously stirred, and Verischenzko watched him narrowly. Anything to do with John must concern Amaryllis, and therefore was of profound interest to himself.

"Not bad news, I hope?" he said.

Denzil was gazing into the fire, and there was a look of wonderment and even rapture upon his face.

"Oh! No—rather splendid . . ."

He felt quite the strangest emotion he had ever experienced in his life. His usual serene self-confidence and easy flow of words deserted him, and Verischenzko, watching him, began to link certain things in his mind.

"Tell me, what did you think of your cousin, Lady Ardayre?" he asked casually, as though the subject were irrelevant.

"Amaryllis?" Denzil almost started from a reverie. "Oh yes, of course—she is a lovely creature, is she not, Stépan?"

Verischenzko narrowed his eyes.

"I have told you that I adore her, but with the spirit. If it were not so, she would appeal very strongly to the flesh. Yes? Did you not feel it?"

"I did."

"Well?"

"Well . . ."

"She is longing to understand life, she is groping. Why do you not set about her education, Denzil?"

"That is the husband's business."

"Not in this case: I consider it yours. You are the right mate for her. John Ardayre is a good fellow, but he stands for nothing in the affair.

"And why did you waste your time upon Harietta when time is so short?"

"I was given no choice."

"But afterwards, in the hall?"

It was quite evident to Verischenzko that the mention of Amaryllis was causing his friend some unexplainable emotion.

"You did not even exert yourself then. Why, Denzil?"

Denzil lit a cigarette.

"I thought her awfully attractive. It was the first time I had ever seen her, as you know."

"And that was a reason for remaining silent and as stiff as a poker in manner! You English are a strange race!"

Denzil smiled. If Stépan only knew everything, what would he say?

"You were made for each other. If I were you, I would not lose a second's time!"

"My dear old boy, you seem quite to forget that the girl has a husband of her own!"

"Not at all. It is for that reason, just because

of that husband. And I shall say no more, for you are quite intelligent enough to understand."

"You think it is all right then for a woman to have a lover? And you consider that I am quite at liberty to make love to Amaryllis Ardayre?"

"Quite!"

Denzil threw his cigarette end into the fire.

"Well, for once you are wrong, Stépan, in your usually perfect deductions."

He got up from his chair.

"There is a reason in this case which makes the thing an absolute impossibility—under no possible circumstance while John is alive could I make the smallest advance towards Amaryllis! There is another point of honour involved in the affair."

Verischenzko felt that here was some mystery which he had yet to elucidate. The links in the chain were visible up to a point, but he then became baffled by the incontestable fact that Denzil had seen Amaryllis that evening for the first time!

"If that is so, then it is a very great pity," he announced after a moment or two of thought.

"Were the times normal, we might leave all to Fate and trust to luck. But if you are killed and John is killed, it will be a thousand pities for Ferdinand to be the head of the family.

"A creature like that will not enlist; he will be safe while you risk your lives."

Denzil went over to the window, apparently to get out a fresh box of cigars which were in a cabinet nearby.

"John writes tonight that there is the chance of an heir after all, so perhaps we need not worry," he said, his voice a little hoarse with feeling. "I was so awfully glad to hear this, as we all loathe the thought of Ferdinand."

Verischenzko actually was startled, and also he was strangely moved.

"When I saw my lady Amaryllis tonight that idea came to me—only as I believed it was quite an impossibility, I dismissed it. It is a war miracle then?" He smiled enquiringly.

"Apparently."

The cigar-box was selected and Denzil had once more resumed his seat in a big chair before either of them spoke again.

"I perfectly understand that there is some mystery here, Denzil, and that you cannot tell me, and equally I cannot ask you any questions, but it may be that in the days that are coming I could be of assistance to you.

"I have some very curious information which I am holding concerning Ferdinand Ardayre and his activities. You can always count on me. . . ."

Verischenzko rose from his chair, stirred deeply with the thoughts which were coursing through his brain.

"Denzil, I love that woman, and I am absolutely determined that I shall not do so in any way but in spirit. I long for her to be happy—protected. She has an exquisite soul. I would have given her to you with contentment. You are her counterpart upon this plane."

Denzil remained silent. He had never seen Stépan so agitated. The situation was altogether very unusual.

"Do you think Ferdinand will make some protest then?" he asked.

"It is possible."

"But there is absolutely nothing to be said; the fact of there being a child refutes all the old rumours."

"In law . . ."

"In every way." A flush had mounted to Denzil's forehead.

"You know Lemon Bridges?" Verischenzko suggested.

"Yes. Why do you ask?"

"He is a remarkably clever surgeon. It is said that he is also a gentleman. If this news surprises him, he probably will not express his feelings."

Stépan was observing his friend with the minutest scrutiny now, while he spoke lazily once more as though bent upon a casual topic, and he saw that a lightning flash of anxiety passed through Denzil's eyes.

"I do not see how anyone can have a word to say about the matter," he said, and he lit his cigar deliberately. "John is awfully pleased."

"And so am I, and so are you, and so will be the Lady Amaryllis. Thus, we can only wish for general happiness, and not anticipate difficulties which may never occur. When is the event to happen?"

"The beginning of next May," Denzil announced without hesitation, and then the flush deepened, for he suddenly remembered that John had not mentioned any date in his letter!

The subject was growing embarrassing, and he asked, so as to change it:

"What is your friend *Madame* Boleski doing now, Stépan?"

"She is receiving news from Germany, which I try to make sure she transmits to me. I have, however, some suspicion that she is transmitting back to Germany any information which she can pick up here, but I cannot yet be sure.

"When I am, then I shall have no mercy. She would betray any country for an hour's personal pleasure or gain. I have not yet discovered who the man was at the Ardayre Ball. I told you about it. Just then more important matters pressed and I could not follow up the clue."

"She is certainly physically attractive, and all the things she says are so obvious and easy, and she is quite a rest at a dinner, but Lord!" Denzil smiled. "Think of spending one's life with a woman like that!"

"There are very few women whom it would be possible to contemplate in calmness spending one's life with, because one's own needs change, and the woman's also!"

Denzil laughed aloud.

"You are hard on us, Stépan, but I dare say you are right."

"I must leave you now, old man," Verischenzko said suddenly, looking at his watch. "I have a rendezvous with Harietta. I shall have to play the part of an ardent lover, and cannot yet wring her neck."

When Denzil was alone, he stood gazing into the fire.

'John would take care of Amaryllis,' he was thinking, but John was going out to fight, and so was he, and they might both be killed.

What then?

'Stépan knows, I am certain,' he thought, 'and he is true as steel; he must stand by her if we don't come back.'

And then his thoughts flew to the vision of her sitting opposite him at the table, with her sweet eyes turned to his.

He knew the faint violet shadows beneath them, and the transparent exquisiteness of her skin told their own story of her fragile beauty.

Oh, what unutterable joy to hold her in his arms and whisper passionate love-words in her little ears, to live again the dream of her dainty head lying prone there on his breast. Every pulse in his being throbbed to bursting, seeming almost to suffocate him.

"Amaryllis—sweetheart!" he whispered aloud, and then started at his own voice.

He paced up and down the room, clenching his hands. The family might go on, but two members of it must endure the pain of renunciation.

Which was the harder to bear, he wondered: his part of hopeless memory and regret, or John's of forced denial and abstinence?

In all the world, no situation could be more strange or more cruel.

He had felt deeply about it before he had seen Amaryllis.

He thought of the myth of Eros and Psyche: his emotions had been much as Psyche's before she lit the lamp.

And now the lamp had been lighted, his eyes had seen what his arms had clasped, the reality was more lovely than his dream, and passion was kindled a hundredfold.

It swept him off his feet.

He forgot war and the horror of the time. He forgot everything except that he longed for Amaryllis.

"She is mine, absolutely mine," he said wildly; "not John's."

And then he remembered his promise, given before any personal equation had entered into the affair.

Never to take advantage of the situation afterwards!

And what would the child be like? A true Ardayre, of course. They would say that it had harked back, perhaps, to that Elizabethan Denzil whom his father had told him was his exact portrait in the picture gallery at Ardayre.

He could have laughed at the sardonic humour of everything if he had not been too overcome with passionate desire to retain any critical sense.

Then he sat down and forced himself to realise what parenthood meant. Not much to a man as a rule.

He had looked upon those occult stirrings of the spirit of which he had read as romantic nonsense.

It was a natural thing and all right if a man had a place for him to wish to have a son, but otherwise sentimentality over such things was such rot!

And yet now he found himself thrilling with sentiment. He would like to talk to Amaryllis about it, and listen to her thoughts too.

And then he remembered the many discussions with Verischenzko upon the theory of rebirth and of the soul's return again and again until its lessons are learned on this plane of existence.

He wondered what soul would animate the physical form of this little being who would be John's and hers.

And suddenly in his mental vision the walls of the room seemed to fade, and he was only conscious of a vastness of space.

He knew that for this brief moment he was looking into eternity and realising for the first time the wonder of things.

*   *   *

Meanwhile, Verischenzko had returned to the Carlton and was softly walking down the passage towards the Boleskis' rooms.

The ante-room door was at the corner, and as he was about ten yards from it a man came out and strode rapidly towards the lift at right angles down the corridor.

The bright light fell upon his face for an instant, and Verischenzko saw that it was Ferdinand Ardayre.

He waited where he was until he heard the lift doors shut, and even then he paced up and down for a time before he entered the sitting-room.

There must be no suspicion that he had encountered the late visitor.

"Darling brute! So here you are!" Harietta cried delightedly, rising from her sofa and throwing herself into his arms.

"I've packed Stanislass off to the St. James's to play piquet. I have been all alone, waiting for you for the last hour. I began to fear you would not come."

Verischenzko looked at her with his cynical, humorous smile, whose meaning never reached her.

He took in the transparent garments which hardly covered her, and then he bent and picked up a man's handkerchief which lay on a table near.

"*Tiens!* Harietta!" he remarked lazily. "Since when has Stanislass taken to using this very Eastern perfume?"

He sniffed with disgust.

The wide look of startled innocence grew in *Madame* Boleski's hazel eyes.

"I believe Stanislass must have got a mistress, Stépan. I have noticed lately these scents on his things. As you know, he never used any before!"

"The handkerchief is marked with 'F.A.' I suppose the *blanchisseuse* mixes them in hotels.

"Let us burn the memento of a husband's

straying fancies then; the taste in perfumes of his inamorata is anything but refined!"

Verischenzko tossed the bit of cambric into the fire which sparkled in the grate.

"I've lots of news to tell you, darling brute, but I shan't . . . yet! Have you come to England to see that bit of bread and butter, or . . . ?"

But Verischenzko, with a fierce savagery which she adored, crushed her in his arms.

Chapter
Five

On the Tuesday morning after the Carlton dinner, fate fell upon Denzil and Amaryllis in the way the jade does at times, swooping down upon them suddenly and then like a whirlwind altering the very current of their destiny.

It came about quite naturally too, and not by one of those wildly improbable situations which often prove to be stranger than fiction.

Amaryllis was settled in an empty compartment of the Weymouth express at Paddington.

She had said good-bye to John the evening before, and he had returned to camp.

She was going back to Ardayre, and feeling very miserable. Everything had been a disillusion.

John's reserve seemed to have augmented and she had been unable to break it down, and all the new emotions which she was trembling with and longing to express had grown chilled.

Presumably, John must be pleased at the possibility of having a son, since it was his heart's desire; but it almost seemed as though the subject embarrassed him!

And all the beautiful things which she had

meant to say to him about it remained unspoken.

He was stolidly matter-of-fact.

What could it all mean?

At last she had become deeply hurt, and had cried with a tremor in her voice the morning before he had left her:

"Oh, John, how different you have become. It can't be the same you who once called me 'sweetheart' and held me so closely in your arms.

"Have I done anything to displease you, dearest? Aren't you glad that I am going to have a baby?"

He had kissed her and assured her gravely that he was glad—overjoyed. And his eyes had been full of pain, and he had added that he was stupid and dull, but that she must not mind, it was only his way.

She dwelt upon these things as she sat in the train, gazing out the window on the blank side.

Yes. Joy was turning into Dead Sea fruit. How moving her thoughts had been when coming up to meet him!

The marvel of love creating life had exalted her, and she had longed to pour her tender visionings into the ears of . . . her lover! For John had been thus enshrined in her fond imagination.

The whole idea of having a child to her was a sacred wonder, with little of earth in it.

She had woven exquisite sentiment round it, and had dreamed fair dreams of how she would whisper her thoughts to John as she lay clasped to his heart.

And John too would be thrilled with exaltation, for was not the glorious mystery his as well . . . not hers alone!

Now everything looked grey.

Tears rose in her eyes. Then she took herself to task; it was perhaps only her foolish romance leading her astray once more.

The thought might mean nothing to a man beyond the pride of having a son to carry on his name. If the baby should be a little girl, John might not care for it at all.

The tears brimmed over and fell upon a big crimson carnation in her coat, a bunch of which John had ordered to be sent her, and which were now safely reposing in a cardboard box in the rack above her head.

Fortunately, she had the carriage to herself. No one had attempted to get in, and they would soon be off.

To be away from London would be a relief.

Then her thoughts flew to Verischenzko.

He had told her that circumstances in his country might require his frequent presence in England for the next few months.

She would see him again. What would he tell her to do now? Conquer emotion, assuredly, and look at things with common sense.

The picture of the dinner at the Carlton then came back to her, and the face of Denzil across the table, so like and yet so unlike John!

If Denzil had a wife, would he be cold to her? Was it in the nature of all Ardayres?

At the very instant the train began to move, the carriage was invaded by a man in khaki.

He bounded in and almost fell by her knees, and with a cheery "Just done it, Sir!" the guard flung in a dressing-bag and slammed the door.

She realised with conscious interest that the intruder was Denzil Ardayre!

"How do you do? By Jove! I am awfully sorry." And he held out his hand.

"I nearly lost the train, and I am afraid I have

bundled in without asking leave. I am going down to Bath to say good-bye to my mother. I say, do forgive me if I startled you."

He looked full of concern.

Amaryllis laughed. She was nervous and overstrung.

"Your entrance was certainly sudden, and this is a nonstop to Westbury so we shall have to put up with each other till then. Shall you mind?"

"Awfully. Must I say that the truth would be that I am enchanted!"

Fortune had flung him these two hours, he had not planned them; his conscience was clear, and he could not help delight rushing through him.

Two hours with her—alone!

There are some blue eyeys which seem to have a spark of the devil always lurking in them, even when they are serious. Denzil's were such eyes.

Women found it difficult to resist his charm, and indeed had never tried very hard!

Life and its living, knowledge to acquire, work to do, and beasts to hunt, had not left him, fortunately, too much time to be spoiled by them, and he had passed through several adventures safely.

He had never felt anything but the most transient emotion, until now, looking at Amaryllis sitting opposite him, he knew that he was in love with this dream which had materialised.

Amaryllis studied him while they talked of ordinary things and the war news, and when he would go out.

She felt some strong attraction drawing her to him. Her sense of depression left her.

She found herself noticing how the sun, which had broken through a cloud, turned his immaculately brushed hair to bronze.

Everything in Denzil was in the right place, she decided, and, above all, he looked so peculiarly alive.

He seemed indeed to be the reality of what her imagination had built up round the personality of John in the weeks of their separation.

Denzil believed that he was talking quite casually, but his glance was ardent, and atmosphere becomes charged when emotions are strong, no matter how insignificant words may be.

Amaryllis *felt* that he was deeply interested in her.

"You know my friend Verischenzko well, it seems," she said presently. "Is he not a fascinating creature? I always feel stimulated when I am with him, and as if I must accomplish great things."

"Stépan is a wonder. We were at Oxford together. He can do anything he desires. He is a musician and an artist, and is full of common sense, and there's not a touch of rot. He would have taken Honours if he had not been sent down."

Amaryllis wanted to know about this, and listened, amused, to the story of the mad freak which had so scandalised the dons.

She had recovered from her nervousness. She was natural and delightful, and although the peculiar situation was filling Denzil with excitement and emotion, he was too much a man-of-the-world to experience any *gêne*.

So they talked for a while with friendliness upon interesting things.

Then a pause came and Amaryllis looked out the window, and Denzil had time to grow aware that he must hold himself with a tighter hand, for a sense almost of intoxication had begun to steal over him.

Suddenly Amaryllis grew very pale and her eyelids flickered a little: for the first time in her life she felt faint.

He bent forward in anxiety as she leaned her head against the cushioned division.

"Oh, what is it, you poor little darling? What can I do for you?" he exclaimed, unconscious that he had used a word of endearment.

But even though things had grown vague for her, Amaryllis caught the tenderly pronounced "darling," and, physically ill as she felt, her spirit thrilled with some agreeable surprise.

He came nearer, and, pushing up the padded division between the seats, he lifted her as though she were a baby and laid her flat down.

He got out his flask from his dressing-bag and poured some brandy between her pale lips, then he rubbed her hands, murmuring he knew not what of commiseration.

She looked so fragile and helpless, and the probable reason of her indisposition was of such infinite solicitude to himself.

'To think that she is feeling like that because . . . Ah! And I may not even kiss her and comfort her, or tell her I adore her and understand,' he thought to himself.

Presently Amaryllis sat up and opened her eyes.

She had not actually fainted, but for a few moments everything had grown dim and she was not certain of what had happened, or if she had dreamed that Denzil had spoken a love-word, or whether it was true.

"I did feel so queer," she said, and smiled feebly. "How silly of me! I have never felt faint before. It is stupid."

She blushed deeply, remembering what certainly must have been the cause.

"I am going to open the window wide," he said, appreciating the blush, and let it down.

"You ought not to sit with your back to the engine like that. Let us change sides."

He took command and drew her to her feet, and placed her gently in his vacant seat; then he sat down opposite her and looked at her with anxious eyes.

"I sit that way as a rule because of avoiding the dust, but of course it was that. I am not generally such a goose though; it is the nastiest feeling that I have ever known."

"You poor, dear little girl," he said in a deep voice. "You must just shut your eyes and not talk now."

She obeyed, and he watched her intently as she lay back with her eyes closed, the long lashes resting upon her pale cheeks.

She looked childish and a little pathetic, and every fibre of his being quivered with desire to protect her.

He had never felt so profoundly in his life, and the whole thing was so complicated.

He tried to force himself to remember that he was not travelling with *his* wife, whom he could take care of and cherish because she was going to have *his* child, but that he was travelling with John's wife, whom he hardly knew, and must take no more interest in her than any other Ardayre would in the wife of the head of the family!

He could have laughed at the extraordinary irony of the thing, if it had not been so moving.

Amaryllis was only conscious that Denzil seemed the reality of her dream of John, and that she liked his nearness, and Denzil only knew that he loved her extremely and must banish emotion and remember his given word.

So he pulled himself together when she sat up presently and began talking again, and gradually the atmosphere of throbbing excitement between them calmed.

They spoke of each other's tastes and likings, and found many to be the same; then they spoke of books, and each discovered that the other was sufficiently well read to be able to discuss varied favourite authors.

An understanding and sympathy had grown up between them before they reached Westbury, and yet Denzil was really trying to keep his word in the spirit as well as the letter.

Amaryllis felt no constraint. She was more friendly than she would have been with any other man she knew so slightly. Were they not cousins, and was it not perfectly natural!

He longed to ask her many questions, and then a pang of jealousy shook him. She would confide to John, not to him, all the emotions aroused by the thought of the child.

Then he wondered what she would do in the winter all alone.

Had she relations she was fond of?

He wished that she knew his mother, who was the kindest, sweetest lady in the world.

"I would like you to meet my mother," he said aloud. "She is going to be at Bath for a month. She is almost an invalid, with rheumatism in her ankle, where she broke it five years ago. I believe you would get on."

"I should love to. It is not an impossible distance from us. I will go over to see her, if you will tell her about me, so that she won't think some stranger is descending upon her someday!"

"She will be so pleased," he said, and he thought that he would be happier knowing that they were friends.

"Does she mean a great deal to you? Some mothers do."

And she signed, for her own was less than an emptiness; they had never been close, and now her step-father and the step-family claimed all the affection her mother could feel.

"She is a great dear, one of my best friends," he said, his eyes beaming. "We have always been pals because I have no brothers and sisters. I suppose she spoilt me!"

"I dare say you were quite a nice little boy!" Amaryllis smiled. "And it must be divine to have a son. I expect it would be easy to spoil one."

Denzil clasped his hands rather tightly; she looked so adorable as she said that, her eyes soft with inward knowledge of her great hope.

How impossible it all was that they must remain strangers, casual cousins and nothing more.

"It must be an awful responsibility to have children," he said, watching her. "Don't you think so?"

The pink flared up again as she answered a rather solemn "Yes."

Then she went on, a little hurriedly:

"One would try to study their characters and lead them to the highest good, as gardeners watch over and train plants until they come to perfection. But what funny, serious things we are talking about."

She gave a nervous little laugh.

"Like two old grandfather philosophers."

"It is rather a treat to talk seriously; one so seldom has the chance to meet anyone who understands."

"To understand!" She sighed. "Alas, how quite perfect life would be . . ."

But she stopped abruptly. If she continued, her words might contain a reflection upon John.

Denzil bent forward eagerly. What had she been going to say?

She saw his blue attractive eyes gazing at her so ardently and some delicious thrill passed through her.

But Denzil recovered himself and leaned back in his seat, while he abruptly changed the conversation by remarking casually:

"I have never seen Ardayre. I would love to look at our common ancestors. My father used to say there was an Elizabethan Denzil who was rather like me. I suppose we are all stamped with the same brand."

"I know him!" Amaryllis cried delightedly. "He is up at the end of the gallery in puffed white satin and a ruff. Of course you must come and see him. He has exactly the same eyes."

"The whole family are alike, I believe: we were a tenacious lot!"

"If you and John both get leave at Christmas you must come with him and spend it at Ardayre. I shall have made your mother's acquaintance by then, and we must persuade her too."

He gave some friendly answer, while he felt that John might not endorse this invitation. If the places were reversed, how would he himself act?

Difficult as the situation was for him, it was infinitely harder for John.

Then the train stopped at Westbury.

Denzil got out to get some papers which he

had been too hurried to secure at Paddington, tipping the guard on the way, so that an old gentleman who showed signs of desiring to enter was warded off to another compartment!

Thus, when the train restarted they were again left alone.

Amaryllis had partially recovered and was looking nearly her usual self but for the violet shadows beneath her eyes.

She glanced at the papers which he handed to her, and Denzil retired behind *The Times*.

He wanted to think; he must not let himself slip out of hand. He must resolutely stamp out all the emotion that she was causing him: he despised weakness of any sort.

He had had his indulgence in the two hours to Westbury, and had very nearly let it conquer him, more than once, and now he must not only curb all friendly words and delightful dalliance with forbidden topics, but he must also feel no more passion.

He made himself read the war news and try to visualise the grim reality behind the official phrasing of the *communiqués*.

And gradually he became calm, and was almost startled when Amaryllis, who had been watching him furtively and had begun to wonder if he was really so interested in his paper, said timidly:

"Will you pull the window down a little? It seems to be growing cold."

She noticed that his lips were set firmly and that an abstracted expression had grown in his eyes.

Then Denzil spoke, now quite naturally about the war, and deliberately kept the conversation to this subject, until Amaryllis lay back again in her corner and closed her eyes.

"I am going to have a little sleep," she said.

She too had begun to realise that in more personal investigation of mutual tastes there lay some danger.

She had become conscious of the fact that she was very interested in Denzil, and that he was not really the least like John!

They were silent for some time, and were nearing Frome when he spoke.

He had been deliberating as to what he ought to do. Get out and leave her, to catch his connexion to Bath, or sacrifice that and see her safely to her destination, and perhaps hire a motor from Bridgeborough?

This latter was his strong desire and also seemed the only chivalrous thing to do when she still looked so pale, but . . .

"Here we are almost at Frome," he said.

Her eyes rounded with concern. It would be horrid to be alone. She had left her maid in London for a few days' holiday.

"You change here for Bath," she said, and faltered a little uncertainly.

He decided in a second. He could not be inhuman! Duty and desire were one!

"Yes, but I am coming on with you. I shall not leave you until I see you safely into your own motor. I can hire one perhaps then, to take me on the rest of the way."

She was relieved; or she thought it was merely relief which made a sudden lifting in her heart!

"How kind of you. I do feel as if I did not like the thought of being by myself. It is so stupid of me.

"But you can't hire a motor from Bridgeborough which would get you to Bath before dark; they are wretched things there.

"You must come with me to Ardayre. It is on the Bath road, you know. And we can have a late lunch, and then I'll send you on in the Rolls-Royce. You will be there in an hour: in time for tea."

This was a tremendous fresh temptation. He tried to look at it as though it did not in reality matter to him more than the appearance suggested.

Had there been no emotion in his interest in Amaryllis, he would not have hesitated, he knew.

Then it was only for him to conquer emotion and behave as he would do under ordinary circumstances. It would be a good test of his will.

"All right, that's splendid, and I shall be able to see Ardayre!"

It was when they were in Amaryllis's own little coupé, very close to each other, that strong temptation assailed Denzil.

He suddenly felt his pulses throbbing wildly, and it was with the greatest difficulty that he prevented himself from clasping her in his arms.

He tried to look out the window and take an interest in the park, which was entered very soon after leaving the station.

He told himself Ardayre was something which deserved his attention, and he looked for the first view of the house; but all his will could only keep his arms from transgressing, it could not control the riot of his thoughts.

Amaryllis was conscious in some measure that he was far from calm, and her own heart began to beat unaccountably.

She talked rather fast about the place and its history, and both were relieved when the front door came in sight.

There was a welcoming smell of burning logs in the hall to greet them, and the old butler could not restrain an expression of startled curiosity when he saw Denzil, for the likeness to his master was so great.

"This is Captain Ardayre, Filson," Amaryllis said, "Sir John's cousin." And then she gave the order about the motor to take Denzil on to Bath.

They went through the Henry VII inner hall and on to the green drawing-room, with its air of home and comfort, in spite of its great size and stateliness.

There were no portraits here, but some fine specimens of the Dutch school, and the big tawny dogs rose to welcome their mistress and were introduced to their "new relation."

She was utterly fascinating, Denzil thought, playing with them there on the great rug.

"We shall lunch at once," she told him, "and then rush through the pictures afterwards before you start for Bath."

They both tried to talk of ordinary things for the few moments before the meal was announced, and then some kind of devilment seemed to come into Amaryllis.

Nothing could have been more seductive or alluring than her manner, while keeping to strict convention.

The bright pink colour glowed in her cheeks and her eyes sparkled.

She could not have accounted for her mood herself. It was one of excitement and interest.

Denzil had the hardest fight he had ever been through, and he grew almost gruff in consequence. He was really suffering.

He admired the way she acted as hostess, and the way the house was done.

He hardly felt anything else, though apart from her he would have been interested in his first view of Ardayre, but she absorbed all other emotions.

He only knew that he desired to make passionate love to her, or to get away as quickly as he could.

"Are you going to remain here all the winter?" he asked her presently, as they rose from the table. "Or shall you go to London? You will be awfully lonely, won't you, if you stay here?"

"I love the country and I am growing to love and understand the place. John wants me to so much. It means more to him than anything else in the world. I shall remain until after Christmas anyway.

"But come now, I want just to take you into the church, because there are two such fine tombs there of both our ancestors, yours and mine.

"We can go out the windows and come back for coffee in the cedar parlour."

Denzil acquiesced; he wished to see the church.

They reached it in a minute or two, and Amaryllis opened the door with her own key and led him on up the aisle to the recumbent knights, and then she whispered their history to him, standing where a ray of sunlight turned her brown hair to gold.

"I wonder what their lives were," Denzil said, "and if they lived and loved and fought their desires, as we do now. The younger one's face looks as though he had not always conquered his. Stépan would say his indulgences had become his masters, not his servants, I expect."

"Verischenzko is wonderful; he makes one want to be strong," Amaryllis said with a sigh. "I wonder how many of us even begin to fight our desires."

"One has to be strong always if one wants to attain, but sometimes it is only honour which holds one, and weaklings are so pitiful."

"What is honour?"

Her eyeys searched his face wistfully.

"Is it being true to some canon of the laws of chivalry, or is it being true to some higher thing in one's own soul?"

Denzil leaned against the tomb, and he thought deeply; then he looked straight into her eyes and said:

"Honour lies in not betraying a trust reposed in one, either in the spirit or in the letter."

"Then, when we say of a man 'he acted honourably,' we mean that he did not betray a trust placed in him, even if it was only perhaps by circumstance and not by a person."

"It is simply that, keeping faith.

"If a man stole a sum of money from a friend, the dishonour would not be in the act of stealing, which is another offence, but in abusing his friend's trust in him by committing that act."

"Dishonour is a betrayal, then."

"Of course."

"Why would this knight," and she placed her hand on the marble face, "have said that he must kill another who had stolen his wife, say, to avenge his 'honour'?"

"That is the conventional part of it, what Stépan calls the grafting on of a meaning to suit some idea of civilisation. It was a nice way of having personal revenges too, and teaching people that they could not steal anything with impunity.

"If we analysed that kind of honour we would find it was principally vanity. The dishonour really lay with the wife, if she deceived her husband, and with the other man if he were the husband's friend.

"If he were not, his abduction of the woman was not 'dishonourable,' because he was not trusted; it was merely an act of theft."

"What then must we do when we are very strongly tempted?"

Her voice was so low he could hardly hear it.

"It is sometimes wisest to run away."

And he turned from her and moved towards the door.

She followed, wondering. She knew not why she had promoted this discussion. She felt that she had been very unbalanced all the day.

They went back to the house almost silently and through the green drawing-room window again, then up the broad stairs with Sir William Hamilton's huge decorative painting of an Ardayre group of his time filling one vast wall at the turn.

And so they reached the cedar parlour, and found coffee waiting.

There was a growing tension between them, and each guessed that the other was not calm.

Amaryllis began showing him the view from the windows across the park, and then the old fireplace and panelling of the room.

"We sit here generally when we are alone," she said. "I like it the best of all the rooms in the house."

"It is a fitting frame for you."

Denzil had many things he longed to say to her of the place, and the thoughts it called up in him, but he checked himself. The thing was to get through with it all quickly and to be gone.

They went into the picture gallery then, and began from the end, and when they came to the Elizabethan Denzil they paused for a little while.

The painted likeness was extraordinary to the living splendid namesake who gazed up at the old panel with such interested eyes.

'If only John had that something in him

which these two have in their eyes, how happy we could be,' Amaryllis thought.

And Denzil was thinking:

'I hope the child will reproduce the type.'

He felt it would be some kind of satisfaction to himself if she should have a son which should be his own image.

"It is so strange," she remarked, "that you should be exactly like this Denzil, and yet resemble John, who does not remind me of him at all, except in the general family look which every one of them shares. This one might have been painted from you."

He looked down at her suddenly and he was unable to control the passionate emotion in his eyes.

He was thinking that, yes, certainly the child must be like him—and then what message would it convey to her?

Amaryllis was disturbed. She longed to ask him what it was which she felt, and why there seemed some elusive remembrance always haunting her.

She grew confused, and they passed on to another frame, which contained the Lady Amaryllis who had had the sonnets written to her nut-brown locks. She was a dainty creature in her stiff farthingale, but bore no likeness to the present mistress of Ardayre.

Denzil examined her for some seconds, and then he said reflectively:

"She is a sweetheart, but she is not you!"

There was some tone of tenderness in his voice when he said the word "sweetheart," and Amaryllis started and drew in her breath.

It recalled something which had given her joy, a low murmur whispered in the night.

"Sweetheart!" A word which John, alas, had never used before or since, except in that one letter in answer to her cry of exultation, her glad Magnificat.

What was this echo sounding in her ears?

How like was Denzil's voice to John's, only a little deeper.

Why, why should he have used that word "sweetheart"?

No coherent thought had yet come to her; it was as though she had looked for an instant upon some scene which awakened a chord of memory, and then the curtain had dropped before she could define it.

She grew agitated, and Denzil, turning, saw that her face was pale and her grey eyes vague and troubled.

"I am quite sure that it is tiring you, showing me all the house like this. We won't look at another picture, and really I must be getting on."

She did not contradict him.

"I am afraid that perhaps you ought to go if you want to arrive by daylight."

And as they returned to the green drawing-room she said some nice things about wanting to meet his mother, and she tried to be natural and at ease, but her hand was as cold as ice when he held it in saying good-bye, after Filson had announced the motor.

And if his eyes had shown passionate emotion in the picture gallery, hers now filled with question and distress.

"Good-bye, Denzil . . ."

"Good-bye, Amaryllis."

He could not bring himself to say the usual conventionalities, and went towards the door with nothing more.

Her brain was clearing; terror and passion and uncertainty had come in like a flood.

"Denzil!"

Her face had paled still further, and there was an anguish of pleading in it.

"Oh, please, what does it all mean?" she cried; and then she fell forward in his arms.

He held her breathlessly. Had she fainted? No, she still stood on her feet, but her little face there lying on his breast was as a lily in whiteness, and tears escaped from her closed eyes.

"For God's sake, Denzil, have you not something to tell me? You cannot leave me so!"

He shivered with the misery of things.

"I have nothing to tell you, child."

His voice was hoarse.

"You are overwrought and overstrung. I have nothing to say to you but just good-bye."

She held his coat and looked up at him wildly.

"Denzil . . . it was you . . . not . . . John!"

He unclasped her clinging arms.

"I must go."

"You shall not until you answer me. I have a right to know."

"I tell you I have nothing to say to you."

He was stern with the suffering of restraint.

She clung to him again.

"Why did you say that word 'sweetheart' then? It was your own word. Oh, Denzil, you cannot be so frightfully cruel as to leave me in uncertainty. . . . Tell me the truth or I shall die!"

But he drew himself away from her and was silent.

He could not make lying protestations of not understanding her, so there only remained one course for him to follow: he must go, and the brutality of such action made him fierce with pain.

She burst into passionate sobs, and would have fallen to the ground, but he raised her in his arms and laid her on the sofa near. And then fear seized him.

What if this excitement and emotion should make her really ill?

He knelt down beside her and stroked her hair. But she only sobbed the more.

"How hideously cruel are men. Why can't you tell me what I ask you? You dare not even pretend that you do not understand!"

He knew that his silence was an admission. He was torn with distress.

"Darling," he cried at last in torment, "for God's sake, let me go!"

"Denzil . . ."

And then her tears stopped suddenly, and the great drops glistened on her white cheeks. Weeping had not disfigured her; she looked but as a suffering child.

"Denzil, if you knew everything you could not possibly leave me. You don't know what has happened. But you must, you will have to, since . . . soon . . ."

He bowed his head and placed her two hands over his face with a despairing movement.

"Hush, I implore you. Say nothing. I do know, and I love you . . . but I must go."

At that she gave a glad cry and drew him close to her.

"You shall not now! I do not care for conventions any more, or for laws, or for anything! I am a savage. You are mine. John must know that you are mine!

"The family is all that matters to him; I am only an instrument, a medium for its continuance.

"But, Denzil, you and I are young and loving and living. It is you I desire, and now I know that I belong to you. You are the man and I am the woman . . . and the child will be our child!"

Her spirit had arisen at last and broken all chains.

She was transfigured, transformed, translated. No one knowing the gentle Amaryllis could have recognised her in this fierce, primitive creature claiming her mate!

Furious, answering passion surged through Denzil. It was the supreme moment when all artificial restrictions of civilisation were swept away. Nature had come to her own.

All her forces were working for these two of her children brought near by a turn of fate.

He strained her in his arms wildly, and he kissed her lips and ears and eyes.

"Mine, mine!" he cried. "Sweetheart!"

And for some seconds, which seemed an eternity of bliss, they forgot all but the joy of love.

But presently reality fell upon Denzil, and he almost groaned.

"I must leave you, precious dear one, even so. I gave my word of honour to John that I would never take advantage of the situation. Fate has done this thing by bringing us together: it has overwhelmed us.

"I do not feel that we are greatly to blame, but that does not release me from my promise. It is all a frightful price that we must pay for pride in the family. Darling, help me to have courage to go."

"I will not. It is shameful cruelty."

She clung to him.

"I am yours really, not John's. Everything in my heart and being cries out to you. You are the reality of my dream-lover; your image has been growing in my vision for months.

"I love you, Denzil, and it is your right to stay with me now and take care of me, and it is my right to tell you of my thoughts about the child. Ah, if you knew what it means to me! The joy, the wonder, the delight!

"I cannot keep it all to myself any longer. I am starving! I am frozen! I want to tell it all to my beloved!"

He held her to him again, and she poured forth the tenderest holy things, and he listened, enraptured, and forgot time and place.

"Denzil," she whispered at last, from the shelter of his arms, "I have felt so strange, exalted, ever since, and now I shall have this ever-present thought of you and love woven in my existence.

"But how is it going to be in the years which are coming? How can I go on pretending to John?

"I cannot. I shall blurt out the truth. For me there is only you; not just the you of these last days since we saw each other with our eyes, but the you that I had dreamed about and fashioned as my lover, my delight.

"Can I whisper to John all my joy and tenderness as I watch the growing of my little one? No, the thing is monstrous, grotesque. I will not face the pain of it all.

"John gave you to me. He must have done so. It was some compact between you both for the family, and if I did not love you I should hate you now, and want to kill myself. But I love you, I love you, I love you!"

She fiercely clasped her arms once more about his neck.

"You must take the consequences of your action. I did not ask to have this complication in my life. John forced it upon me for his own aims, but I have to be reckoned with, and I want my lover; I claim my mate."

Her cheeks were flaming and her grey eyes flashed.

"And your lover wants you."

Denzil wildly returned her fond caress.

"But the choice is not left to me, darling, even if you were my wife, not John's. You have forgotten the war. I must go out and fight."

All the warmth and passion died out of her, and she lay back on the pillows of the sofa for a moment and closed her eyes.

She had indeed forgotten that ghastly colossus, in her absorption in their own two selves.

Yes, he must go out and fight, and John would go too, and they might both be killed like all those gallant partners of the season and her cousin, and those who had fallen at Mons and the Battle of the Marne.

No, she must not be so paltry as to think of personal things, even love. She must rise above all selfishness, and not make it harder for her man.

Her little face grew resigned and sanctified, and Denzil, watching her with burning, longing eyes, waited for her to speak.

"It is true: for the moment nothing but you and my great desire for you was in my mind. But you are right, Denzil, of course I cannot keep you.

"Only I am glad that just this once we have tasted a brief moment of happiness. And, Denzil, I believe our souls belong to each other, even if we do not meet again on earth."

And then at last they parted, and Amaryllis, listening, heard the motor go.

She rose from the sofa and went out through the window to the lawn, and so to the church again, and there she lay on the steps of the young knight's tomb, sobbing and praying until darkness enveloped the land.

Chapter
Six

Just before Denzil sailed for France, he dined with Verischenzko, and he guessed by Denzil's face what had happened when they spoke of Amaryllis.

He knew John was unable to have children, and he surmised what had happened.

He promised he would see Amaryllis at Ardayre and look after her.

But Amaryllis came up to London the following week to say good-bye to John, so Verischenzko did not go down to Ardayre to see her.

John's leave-taking was characteristic: he could not break through the iron band of his reserve. He longed to say something loving to her, but the more deeply he felt things, the greater was his difficulty in self-expression.

And the knowledge of the secret he hid in his heart made him still more ill-at-ease with Amaryllis.

She too was changed, and he felt it at once. Her grey eyes were mysterious; they had grown from a girl's into a woman's.

She did not mention the coming child until

he did, and then it was she who showed desire to change the conversation.

Only she wondered, when she looked at him sitting opposite her, talking gravely about the baby, in the library of Brook Street, how he could possibly be feeling.

What an immense influence the thought of the family must have in his life. She understood it in a great measure herself.

She remembered Verischenzko's words, upon the occasions when he had spoken to her about it, and her duties towards it, and how she must uphold it.

She particularly remembered what he had said when they walked by the lake, and he had seemed to be transmitting some message to her, which she had not understood at the time.

Did Verischenzko know then that John must always be heirless? And had he been suggesting to her that the line should go on through her?

Some of the pride in it all had come to her before she had left the dark church after parting with Denzil.

Perhaps she was fulfilling destiny. She must not be angry with John. She did not try to cease loving Denzil. She had not knowingly been unfaithful to John, and now she would be faithful to Denzil, for he was her love and her mate.

Indeed, even in the fortnight which had elapsed between her farewell to him, and now, when she was going to say farewell to John, she had had many moments of tender consolation in the thought of the baby, Denzil's son.

She could revive and revel in that exquisite exaltation which she had experienced at first and which John had withcred.

Denzil far surpassed even the imagined lover into which she had turned John.

So now Denzil had become the reality and John the dream.

She felt sorry for her husband too. She was fine enough to understand and divine his difficulties.

She found that she felt just nothing for him but a kindly affection.

She knew that her whole being was given to Denzil, who represented her dream.

She tried to be very kind to John, and when he kissed her before starting, the tears came to her eyes.

Poor, good, cold John!

So both Denzil and John went to the war, and Amaryllis was alone.

Verischenzko had returned to Paris without seeing her, and it was the beginning of December before he was in England again and rang her up at Brook Street, where she had returned for a week, asking if he might call.

"Of course," she said; and so he came.

The library was looking its best. Amaryllis had a knack of arranging flowers and cushions and such things, her rooms always breathed an air of home and repose, and Verischenzko was struck by the sweet scent and the warmth and cosiness when he came in out of the gloomy fog.

She rose to greet him, her face more ethereal still than when he had dined with her.

"You are looking like an angel," he said, when she had given him some tea and they were seated on the big sofa before the fire.

"What have you to tell me? I know that you are going to have a child. I am very interested about it all."

Amaryllis blushed a soft pink.

He went on with perfect calm:

"You blush as though I had said something unheard of! You are to be congratulated that you are going to have a baby, do you not think so?"

"Of course I do."

And Amaryllis controlled her uneasy bashfulness. She really wished to talk to her friend.

"Who told you about it?" she asked.

"Denzil."

Amaryllis drew in her breath suddenly. Verischenzko's eyes were looking her through and through.

"Denzil?"

"Yes. He is glad that there may be the possibility of a son for the family."

"Yes."

"How do you feel about it? It is an enormous responsibility to have children."

"I feel that. I want to do the wisest things from the beginning."

"You must take great care of yourself, and always remain serene. Never let your mind become agitated by speculation as to the future; keep all thoughts fixed upon the *now*."

Amaryllis looked at him, a little troubled.

What did he know? Something tangible? Or were these views of his just applicable to any case? Her eyes were full of questions and pleading.

"What do you want to ask me?"

His eyes narrowed in contemplating her.

"I . . . I . . . do not know."

"Yes, you want to hear of Denzil—is it not so?"

She clasped her hands.

"Yes, perhaps . . ."

"He is well. I heard from him yesterday. He

asked me to come to you. His mother is still at Bath, and he wishes you to meet."

Suddenly the impossibility of everything seemed to come over Amaryllis. She rose quickly and threw out her hands.

"Oh, if I could only understand the meaning of things, my friend. I am afraid to think!"

"You love Denzil very much—yes?"

"Yes."

"Sit down and let us talk about it, Lady of My Soul. I am your mother now."

She sank into her seat beside him, among the green silk pillows, and he leaned back and watched her for a while.

"He fulfils some imaginary picture, *hein?* You had not seen him really until we all dined?"

"No."

"You were bound to be drawn to him, he is everything a woman could desire; but it was not only that—tell me?"

"He was what I had hoped John would be; the likeness is so great. . . ."

"It is much deeper than that. Nature was drawing you unconsciously."

She covered her face with her hands. It seemed as if Verischenzko must know the truth.

Had Denzil told him, or was it his wonderful intuition which was enlightening him now, or was it just her sensitive conscience?

Then she asked softly:

"Do you think it is wicked of me to be thinking of Denzil . . . not John?"

"No, it is quite natural. The wickedness would be if you pretended to John that you were thinking of him. Deception is wickedness."

"Everything is so sad now. Both have gone to fight. I do not dare to think at all."

"Yes, you must think. You must think of your child and draw to it all the good forces, so that it may come to life unhampered by any weakness or unbalance in you—that must be your constant self-discipline. Keep serene and try to live in a world of noble ideals and serenity.

"Now I am going to play to you."

Amaryllis had never heard Verischenzko play. He arranged the sofa cushions and made her lie comfortably among them.

Then he went to the piano, and presently it seemed to her that her soul was floating upwards into realms of perfect contentment.

She had never even dreamed of such playing. It was like nothing she had ever heard before. The sounds touched all the highest chords in her spirit.

She did not ask whose was the music. She seemed to know that it was Verischenzko's own, which was just talking to her, telling her to be calm and brave and true.

He played for a whole hour, and at last softly and yet more softly, and when he finished he saw that she was quietly asleep.

A smile as tender as a mother's came into his rugged face, and he stole from the room noiselessly, breathing a blessing as he passed.

And somewhere in France, Denzil and John were thinking of her too, each with great love in his heart.

*　　*　　*

Harietta Boleski was growing dissatisfied with her life and with England, yet Hans insisted upon her staying on.

She wanted to go to Paris. The war was altogether a supreme bore and upset her plans!

She had been so successful, in her obvious

stupid way, that Hans had been able to transmit the most useful information to his country, which had assisted to foil more than one Allied plan.

Harietta saw numbers of old gentlemen who pulled strings at that time, and although they wearied her she found them easier to extract news from than the younger men.

Her method was so irresistible: a direct appeal to the senses, and it hardly ever failed. If only Hans would consent to her returning to Paris, with the help of Ferdinand Ardayre, who was now her slave, she promised wonderful things.

Hans, as a Swedish philanthropic gentleman, had been over to give her instructions once or twice, and at last had agreed to her crossing the Channel.

She told this good news to Ferdinand one afternoon just before Christmas, when he came to see her in London.

"I'm going to Paris, Ferdie, and you must come too. There's no use in your pretending that England matters to you, and you are of such use to us with your branch business in Holland like that."

Ferdinand was a rest to her, almost as good as Hans. She need not be overly refined; she knew that he was on the same level as herself.

He amused her, too, in several ways.

He looked sulky now. It did not suit his plans to go to Paris yet. He was trying to collect information for a game of his own. But where Harietta went, he must go.

He was besotted about her, and knew that he could not trust her a yard.

He protested a little, but, as she never allowed anyone's wishes to interfere with her plans, she only smiled.

"I'm going on Saturday. We have secured a

suite at the Universal this time, now that the Rhin is shut up; and it is such a large hotel you can quite well stay there. Stanislass won't notice you among the crowd."

Ferdinand agreed unwillingly, and just then Verischenzko came in. He had not seem *Madame* Boleski since the night at the Carlton, having taken care not to let her know of his further visits to England since.

He looked at Ferdinand Ardayre as though he were some bit of furniture, and he took up Fou-Chou, who was cowering beneath a chair; he did not speak a word.

Harietta talked for a little while and then she began to feel nervous.

Verischenzko smiled lazily. He was trying an experiment. The interview could not go on like this; Ferdinand Ardayre would certainly have to go.

Now that Verischenzko had come, Harietta ardently wished that he would.

The most venomous hate was arising in Ferdinand's resentful soul. He felt that here was a rival to be dreaded indeed.

He saw that Harietta was nervous: he had never seen her so before. He shut his teeth and determined to stay on.

Verischenzko continued his disconcerting silence. Harietta felt that she should presently scream. She took Fou-Chou from Stépan, and pinched him cruelly in her exasperation. He gave a feeble squeak.

She pushed him roughly down. Animals to her were a nuisance. She disliked them if she had any feeling at all. But Fou-Chou was a coveted possession envied by her many female friends.

Verischenzko raised one bushy eyebrow, and a sardonic smile came into his eyes.

Madame Boleski saw that she had made a

mistake in showing her temper to the dog. It would have given her pleasure then to wring its neck!

The two men sat on. She began to grow so uncomfortable that she could endure it no more.

"You are coming back to dinner, Mr Ardayre," she remarked at length; "and I want you to get some gardenias to wear, if you will be so kind, and I am afraid you will have to hurry, as the shops close soon."

Ferdinand Ardayre rose, rage showing in his mean face, but, as he had no choice, he said goodbye.

Harietta accompanied him to the door, pressing his hand stealthily. Then she returned to the Russian with flaming eyes. He had not uttered a word.

"How dare you make me so nervous? Sitting there like a log! I won't stand for such treatment . . . you hear!"

"Then sit down. Why do you have that Turk with you at all?"

"He is not a Turk, he's an Englishman, and a friend of mine. Why, he is the brother of your precious John Ardayre; and they have behaved shamefully to him, poor dear boy."

She was still enraged.

"He is not even a pure Turk; some of them are gentlemen. He is just the scum of the earth, and no blood relation to John Ardayre."

"He will let them know whether he is or not someday! I hear that your bit of bread and butter is going to have a child, and as Ferdie says it can't be John's, I suppose it is yours!"

Verischenzko's face looked dangerous.

"You would do well to guard your words, Harietta. I do not permit you to make such remarks to me, and it would be more prudent if you warned your friend that he had better not make such assertions either—do you understand?"

Harietta felt some twinge of fear at the strange tone in the Russian's voice, but she was too out of temper to be cowed now.

"Puh!" She tossed her head. "If the child is a boy, Ferdie will have something to say; and as for Amaryllis . . . I hate her! I'd like to kill her with my own hands."

Verischenzko rose and stood before her, and there was a look in his eyes which made her suddenly grow cold.

"Listen," he said icily. "I have warned you once, and you know me well enough to decide whether I ever speak lightly. I warn you again to be careful of your words and your deeds. I shall warn you no more—if you transgress a third time, then I will strike."

Harietta grew pale to her painted lips.

How would he strike? Not with a stick, as Hans would have done, but in some much more deadly way. She changed her manner instantly and began to laugh.

"Darling brute!"

Verischenzko knew that he had alarmed her sufficiently, so he sat down in his chair again and lit a cigarette calmly.

Then he sniffed the air.

"Your mongrel friend uses the same perfume as Stanislass's mistress!"

"Stanislass's mistress?"

She had forgotten for the moment.

"Yes. Don't you remember, we burnt his scented handkerchief the last time we met because we did not like her taste in perfumes."

Harietta's ill-humour rose again; she was annoyed that she had forgotten this incident. Her instinct of self-preservation usually preserved her from committing any such mistakes.

She felt that it was now advisable to become cajoling; also, there was something in the face of Verischenzko and his fierceness which aroused renewed passion in her.

It was absurd to waste time in quarrelling with him when in an hour Stanislass might be coming in, so she went over behind his chair and smoothed back his thick dark hair.

"You know that I adore you, darling brute!"

"Of course."

He did not even turn his head towards her.

"Have you had your heart's desire here in England?"

"Before this stupid war came . . . yes. Now I'm through with it. I'm for Paris again."

"I suppose I must have been mistaken, but I thought I caught sight of your handsome German friend in the hall just now."

"German friend? Who?"

"Your *danseur* at the Ardayre Ball. I have forgotten his name."

"And so have I."

At that instant Marie appeared at the door and Fou-Chou came from under the chair where he was sheltering and pattered towards her with a glad tiny whine.

The maid's eyes rounded with dislike as she looked at her mistress. She realised that the little creature had been roughly treated again.

She picked him up and could hardly control her voice into a tone of respect as she said:

"*Monsieur* Insborg demands if he can see *Madame* in half-an-hour. He telephoned to *Madame* but received no reply."

For a second Harietta's eyes betrayed her, they

narrowed with alarm, and then she said suavely:

"I suppose the receiver was off. No, say I am dining early for the theatre, but tomorrow at five."

The maid inclined her head and left the room silently, carrying Fou-Chou, but as she did so her eyes met Verischenzko's and their expression suggested to him several things.

'Marie loves the dog, so she hates Harietta. Good—we shall see.'

* * *

When Amaryllis knew that John was going to get a few days' leave at Christmas, a strange nervousness took possession of her.

The personality of Denzil had been growing more real to her ever since they had parted, in spite of her endeavours to discipline her mind and control all emotion.

The thought of him and the thought of the baby were inseparable and were seldom absent from her consciousness.

All sorts of wonderful emotions held her, and exalted her imagination until she felt that Denzil was part of her daily life; and with the double interest, her love for him grew and grew.

But now she would have to face the fact of living with John again in an intimate relationship.

The morning John was expected to arrive, she had a hard fight with herself. She felt very nervous and ill-at-ease. Above all things, she must not be unkind.

He was bronzed and looked well, and plainly was very glad to see her.

He held her close to him and bent to kiss her lips; but some undefined reluctance came over her, and she moved her head aside.

Something in her resented the caress. Her lips

were now for Denzil and for no other man. It was she who was recalcitrant and turned the conversation to everyday things.

The De la Paule family had been summoned for luncheon, and the afternoon passed among them all, and then the evening and the *tête-à-tête* dinner came.

John knocked at the door of her room while she was dressing.

Her maid had just finished her hair, and she wondered at herself that she should experience a sense of shyness and have to suppress an inclination to refuse to let him come in.

And once, any of these little intimate happenings would have given her joy!

She kept Adams there, and hurried into her tea-gown, and then walked towards the door.

John, who had not spoken much, stood by the fire.

How changed things were: once, he had had to be persuaded and enticed to stay with her at such moments, and now it was he who seemed to desire to do so, and it was she who discouraged his wishes.

In Amaryllis's mind an agitation grew.

What would she say to him presently, if he suggested coming to sleep in her room?

The knowledge in her breast rose as an insurmountable barrier between them.

During dinner she kept the conversation entirely upon his life at the Front, which indeed really interested her. She was not cold or stiff in her manner, but she was unconsciously aloof.

Then they went back into the library, each feeling exceedingly depressed.

When coffee had come and they were quite alone, Amaryllis felt she could not stand the strain, and went to the piano.

She played for quite a long time all the things

she remembered that John liked best. She wanted the music to calm her, and she wanted to gain time.

John sat in one of the monster-sized chairs and gazed into the fire.

Presently she finished a soft chord and got up and came to his side.

He looked up at her and rose from his chair.

"You play so beautifully," he said hastily. "You take one out of oneself.

"Now it is late and the day has been long; let us go to bed, dearest child."

Amaryllis stiffened suddenly: the moment that she dreaded had come.

"I would rather that you slept in your dressing-room. I have ordered that to be prepared."

He looked at her, startled, and then he took her hand.

"Amaryllis, tell me everything. Why are you so changed?"

"I am trying not to be, John."

"You are trying, which proves that you are, if you must try. Please tell me what this means."

She endeavoured to remain calm and not become unhinged.

"It was you yourself who altered me. I came to you all loving and human, and you froze me. There is nothing to be done."

"Yes, there is; you know that I love you."

"Perhaps you do, but the family matters more to you than I do, or anything else in the world."

"That may have been so once, but not now."

His voice throbbed with feeling.

He longed to appeal to her, but he was too honest to seek to soften her through the link of the child; indeed, the thought of it had grown hateful to him. He only knew that he had played for a stake which now seemed worthless.

Amaryllis and her love mattered more than any child.

He clenched his hands tightly; the pain of things seemed hard to bear.

Why had he not broken the thongs of reserve which held him long days ago, and made love to her in words?

But that would have been dishonest. He must at least be true; and he realised now that he had starved her, no matter what his motive had been.

"Amaryllis, tell me everything, please," he said; and he held out his hands and drew her to the sofa and sat down by her side.

She could not control her emotion any longer, and her voice shook as she answered him:

"I know that it was not you ... but Denzil, John, and the baby is his, not yours."

His face altered. He had not been prepared to hear this thing, and he was stunned.

"Ferdinand is an awful possibility to contemplate there at Ardayre, if you have no son," she went on, trying to be more calm, "but do you not think that you might have told me? Surely a woman has the right to select the father of her child."

John could not answer her; he covered his face with his hands.

"You see, it is all pitiful," she continued, her voice deep and broken, with almost a sob in it.

"Denzil is so like you: it was an easy transition to find that I loved him, because I was only loving the imaginary you I had made for myself. I cannot explain myself and do not make any excuse!

"There is something in me, whenever I think of the baby, that draws me to Denzil and makes me remember that night. John, we must just face the situation and try to find some way to avoid as much pain as we can. I hate to think it is hurting you too."

"Did Denzil tell you this?"

His voice was icy-cold.

"No, it came to me suddenly when I heard him say a word:

" 'Sweetheart.' "

And now John's eyes flashed.

"He called you again 'sweetheart'!"

"No, he did not, he used the word simply in speaking of a picture, but I recognised his voice immediately. It is a little deeper than yours."

"When did you see Denzil?"

She told him the exact truth about their meeting and his coming to Ardayre, and how Denzil had endeavoured to keep his word.

"He would never have spoken to me. It was fate which sent him into the train, and then I made him speak. I could not bear it. After I recognised him, I made him admit that it was he.

"Denzil is not to blame. He left immediately, and I have never seen him or heard from him since. It is I alone who must be counted with, John. Denzil will never try to see me again."

"O God, the misery of it all!" John groaned aloud.

"John, I must tell you everything now, while we are talking of these things.

"I love Denzil utterly. I thrill when I think of him. He seems to me my husband, not even only a lover. John, not long ago, when I felt the first movement of the child, I shook with longing for Denzil, and I found myself murmuring his name aloud!

"So you must think what it all means to me, so strongly passionate as I am. But I would never cheat you, John. I had to be honest. I could not go on pretending to be your wife and living a lie."

Tears of agony gathered in John Ardayre's blue eyes and rolled down his cheeks.

He suddenly understood the suffering that she, too, must be undergoing.

What right had he to have taken this young and loving woman and then to have used her for his own aims, however high?

"Amaryllis, you cannot forgive me. I see now that I was wrong."

But the sympathy which she had felt when she had looked at him from the piano welled up again in Amaryllis's heart and drowned all resentment.

She knew that he must be enduring pain greater than hers, so she stretched out her hands to him, and he took them and held them in his.

"Of course I forgive you, John, but I cannot cease loving Denzil; that is the tragedy of the thing. I am his really, not yours, even if I never see him again, and that is why we must not make any pretences.

"John dearest, let us be friends, and live as friends; then everything won't be so hard."

He let her hands drop and got up and paced the room. He was suffering acutely. Must he renounce even the joy of holding her in his arms?

"But I love you, Amaryllis. I love you, dearest child. This is a frightful sacrifice to me; must you insist upon it?"

Then her eyes seemed to flash fire and her cheeks grew rose, and she stood up and faced him.

"I tell you, John, you do not know me. You have seen a well brought up, conventional girl, milk-and-water, ready to obey your slightest will. I had not found myself. I am a creature as primitive and passionate as a savage."

Her breath came in little pants, with her great emotion.

"I *could* not belong to two men; it would utterly degrade me, and then I do not know what I should become. I love Denzil body and soul, and while he lives, no other man shall ever touch me. That is what passion means to me, fidelity to the thing I love!

"He is my beloved and my darling, and I must go away from you altogether and throw off the thought of the family, and implore Denzil to take me when he comes home, if you can't agree to the only terms I can offer you now."

John bowed his head. Life seemed over for him.

Amaryllis came close to him, then she stood on tiptoe and kissed his brow. Her vehemence had died down in her sorrow for his pain.

"John," she whispered softly, "won't you always be my dearest friend? And when the baby comes it will be a deep interest to us both, and you must love it because it is mine and an Ardayre, and the comfort of that must fill our lives.

"I truly believe that you did everything meaning it for the best, only perhaps it is dangerous to play with the creation of life: perhaps that is why fate forced me to know."

John drew her to him, and smoothed the soft brown hair back from her brow and kissed her tenderly, but not on the lips—those, he told himself, he must renounce forevermore.

"Amaryllis," he said, and his voice was still husky, "yes, I will be your friend, darling, and I will love your child. I was very wrong to marry you, but it was not quite hopeless then, and you were so young and splendid and living, and I was growing to love you, and for these reasons I hoped against hope.

"Then when I knew that everything was impossible, I felt that I must make it up to you in every other way I could. I don't know how to put things into words, I always was dull, but I thought if I gratified all your wishes, perhaps . . .

"Ah, I see it was very cruel. Darling, I would have told you the truth presently, but then the war came, and the thought of Ferdinand here drove me mad and it forced my hand."

She looked up at him with her sweet, true eyes. Her one idea now was to comfort him, since she need no longer fear.

"John, if you had explained the whole thing to me, I do not know, perhaps I should have agreed with you; for I too have much of this family pride, and I cannot bear to think of Ferdinand at Ardayre.

"But suppose anything should happen to Ferdinand," she went on, "then Denzil would have been the next heir, and now if the child is a boy . . .

John started.

We neither of us thought of that.

"But nothing is likely to happen to Ferdinand; he won't enlist. It is only you, dear John, who is in danger, and Denzil too. But surely the war cannot go on long now?"

John wondered if he should tell her what he really felt about this, or whether it was wiser to keep her quietly in this hopeful dream of a speedy end.

He decided to say nothing. It was better for her health not to agitate her mind; events would speak for themselves, alas, presently.

He talked quietly then of Ardayre and of his boyhood and of its sorrows.

He was determined to break down his own reserve, and Amaryllis listened interestedly, and gradually some kind of peace and calm seemed to come to them both, and they resolutely banished the thought of the future, and sought only to think of the present.

And then at last John rose and took her hand.

"Go to bed now, dear little girl, and tomorrow I shall have quite conquered all the feelings which could disturb you; and just remember always that I am indeed your friend."

She understood at last the greatness of his sacrifice and the fineness of his soul, and she fell into a passion of weeping and ran from the room.

But John, left alone, sank down into the same chair as he had done once before, on the night he was waiting for Denzil, and, as then, he buried his face in his hands.

The next day they met at breakfast. John had not slept at all and was very pale, and Amaryllis's eyes still showed the deepened violet shadows from much weeping.

But they were both quite calm.

She came over to John and kissed his forehead with gentle tenderness, and then gave him his tea. They tried to talk in a friendly way, as of old, before any new emotions had come into their lives. And gradually the strain became lessened.

They arranged to go out shopping, and John bought Amaryllis a new emerald ring.

"Green is the colour of hope," she said. "I want green, John, because it will make me think of the spring-time and nature, and all beautiful things."

They lunched at a restaurant, and in the afternoon went down to Ardayre. John had many things to attend to and would be occupied all the following day.

There had been no Christmas feasting, but there were gifts to be distributed and various other duties and ceremonies to be gone through, although they had missed the Christmas Day.

Amaryllis tried in every way to be helpful to her husband, and he appreciated her stateliness and sweet manners with all the tenants and people on the estate.

So the four days passed quite smoothly, and the last night of the old year came.

"I don't think that you must sit up for it, dear," John said after dinner. "It will only tire you, and it is always a rather sad moment unless one has a party, as we always had in old days."

Amaryllis went obediently to her room and stayed there, but sleep was far from her eyes.

What was the rest of her life going to be without Denzil?

And what of John?

She tried to force herself from her unhappy impressions by thinking of what she could do presently in the summer, when she would be quite well again, though her greatest work must always be to try to make John happy, if by then he had come home.

She heard him go into his room at about one o'clock, and then she crept noiselessly to her great gilt bed.

John had waited for the New Year by the cedar-parlour fire. The room was so filled with the radiance of Amaryllis that he liked being there.

And he too was thinking of what their new life would be, should he chance to come through.

The ache in his heart would gradually subside, he supposed, but how would he bear the long years, knowing that Amaryllis was thinking of Denzil and longing for him?

And if fate made them meet, what then?

How could he endure to know that these two beings were suffering?

There seemed no clear outlook ahead. But, as he knew only too well, death could hardly fail to intervene, and if it should claim Denzil, then he must console Amaryllis's grief.

But if, happily, it could be he who was taken, then their future path would be clear.

He could not forget the third eventuality, that he and Denzil might both be killed. He thought and thought over them all, and at last he decided to add a letter to his will.

If he should be killed he would ask Denzil to marry Amaryllis immediately, without waiting for the conventional year.

The times were too strenuous, and she must not be left unprotected, and alone with the child.

He got up and began the letter to his lawyer.

> *I request my cousin, Denzil Benedict Ardayre, to marry Amaryllis, my wife, as soon as possible after my death, if he can get leave and is still alive.*
>
> *I confide her to his care and ask them both not to let any conventional idea of mourning stand in the way of these, my urgent last commands. And I ask my cousin Denzil, if he lives through the war, to take great care of the bringing up of my child.*

It seemed to John that the shadow of sorrow was suddenly removed from him, and as though a weight of care had been lifted from his heart. He could not account for the alteration, but he felt no longer sad.

Was it an omen?

Was this New Year going to fulfil some great thing after all?

A divine peace fell upon him, and then a

pleasant sensation of sleep, and he turned out the lights and went softly to his room, and was soon in bed.

And then he slept soundly until late in the morning, and awoke refreshed and serene on New Year's Day.

His leave was up on January 3 and he returned to London, but he would not let Amaryllis undergo the fatigue of accompanying him.

He said good-bye to her there at Ardayre.

They had the most affectionate parting. John never was sentimental, and he went off with brave, cheery words, and every injunction that she was to take the greatest care of herself.

"Remember, Amaryllis, that you are the most precious thing on earth to me, and you must think also of the child."

She promised him that she would carry out all his wishes in this respect and remain quietly at Ardayre until April 1, when perhaps he could get leave again, and then she would go to London for the birth of the baby.

John turned and waved his hand as he went off down the avenue, and Amaryllis watched the motor until it was out of sight, the tears slowly brimming over and running down her cheeks.

She noticed that at the turn in the avenue a telegraph-boy passed the car and came straight on. The wire was not for John, evidently, so she would wait at the door to see.

It proved to be for her, from Denzil's mother, saying that she was *en route* to Dorchester, motoring, and would stop at Ardayre on the chance of finding its mistress at home.

Amaryllis felt suddenly excited; she had often longed for this, and yet in some way she had feared it also. What new emotions might the meeting arouse?

It was quite early after luncheon when Mrs Ardayre was announced. Amaryllis had waited in the green drawing-room, thinking that she would come.

She was playing the piano at the far end when the door opened, and to her astonishment quite a young, small woman came into the room! She was a little lame, and walked with a stick.

For a moment Amaryllis thought she must be mistaken, and rose with a vague but gracious look in her eyes.

Mrs Ardayre held out her hand and smiled.

"I hope you got my telegram in time. I felt I must not lose the opportunity of making your acquaintance. My son has been so anxious for us to meet."

"You . . . you surely can't be Denzil's mother," Amaryllis exclaimed. "He is much too old to be your son!"

Mrs Ardayre smiled again, while Amaryllis made her sit down on the sofa beside her and helped her off with her furs.

"I am forty-nine years old, Amaryllis, if I may call you so, but one ought never to grow old in body. It is not necessary, and it is not agreeable to the eye!"

Amaryllis looked at her carefully in the full side light.

It was the shape of her face, she decided, which gave her such youth. There were no unsightly bones to cause shadows, and the skin was smooth as ivory, and her eyes were bright brown, their expression very humorous as well as kindly, and Amaryllis was drawn to her at once.

They talked about their desire to know each

other, and about the family, and the place, and the war, and at last they spoke of Denzil, and Mrs Ardayre told of what his life was, and his whereabouts now, and then grew retrospective.

"He is the dearest boy in the world," she said. "We have been friends always, and now he will not allow me to be anxious about him. I really think that as far as the frightfulness of things will let him be, he is actually enjoying his life! Men are such queer creatures, they like to fight!"

Amaryllis asked what was her latest news of him, and where he was, and listened interestedly to Mrs Ardayre's replies.

She wondered what Denzil had told his mother about her: probably that she was going to have a child, but nothing more.

They talked in the most friendly way for half-an-hour, and then Amaryllis asked her guest if she would like to come and see the house and especially the picture gallery and the Elizabethan Denzil hanging there.

"It is just my boy!" Mrs Ardayre cried when they stood in front of it. "Eyes and all: they are bold and true and so loving. Oh, my dear child, you can't think what a darling he is.

"From his babyhood every woman adored him. He has that special quality which can wile a bird off a tree."

Amaryllis listened, enchanted.

"Does it not interest you, Amaryllis," Mrs Ardayre went on, "to wonder what your little one, when it comes, will look like?"

"Indeed yes, I am very curious. And how we all hope that it will be a son!"

"Is there a portrait of your husband here? Denzil says they are alike."

"There is one in my sitting-room. Let us go there now and see it."

"But there is no likeness," Mrs Ardayre exclaimed presently, when they had gone to the cedar parlour and were examining the picture of John. "Can you discover it?"

"I thought they were very alike once, but I do not altogether see it now."

Beatrice Ardayre looked up at the portrait of John.

His stolid face did not give her the impression that he could make a woman, and such a fascinating and adorable creature as Amaryllis, passionately in love with him, or fill her with mysterious feelings of emotion about his child!

Now, if it had been Denzil, she could have understood a woman's committing any madness for him, but this stodgy, respectable John . . .

Her bright brown eyes glanced at Amaryllis furtively, and she saw that she was looking up at the picture with an expression of deep melancholy on her face.

There was some mystery here.

She went over again in her mind what Denzil had told her about Amaryllis; it was not a great deal.

He had arrived at Bath that time looking very stern and abstracted, and had mentioned rather shortly that he had come down with the head of the family's wife in the train, and had gone on to Ardayre with her, after meeting them the previous night at dinner for the first time.

He had not been at all expansive; but later in the evening, when they sat by her sitting-room fire, he had suddenly said something which had startled her greatly:

"Mother, I want you to know Amaryllis Ardayre: I am madly in love with her. She is going to have a baby, and she seems to be so alone."

It must be one of those sudden passions, and the idea seemed in some way to jar a little. Denzil, to have fallen in love with a woman whom he knew was going to have a child!

She said something of this to him, and he had turned to her eyes which were full of pain and even reproach.

"Mother, you always understand me. I haven't anything more to say. Only I want you to be really kind to her, and get to know her well."

And he had not mentioned the subject again, but had been very preoccupied during all his three days' visit, which state she could not account for by the fact of the war.

Denzil, she knew, was an enthusiastic soldier, and to be going out to fight would naturally be to him a keen joy.

What did it all mean?

And here was this sweet creature, looking up with melancholy eyes at the portrait of her dull, unattractive husband, whereas they had sparkled with interest when Denzil was the subject of conversation!

Could she too have fallen in love with Denzil in one night at dinner and a journey in the train?

It was all very remarkable.

They had tea together in the green drawing-room, and by that time had become very good friends.

Mrs Ardayre told Amaryllis of the little old manor-house she had in Kent—The Moat, it was called—and of her garden and the pleasure it was to her.

"I hope you will let me show you them one day," she said.

Amaryllis said she would be delighted, and added:

"You will come and see me, won't you? I am going up to our house in Brook Street at the beginning of April, and I am praying that I may have a little son about the first week in May."

Just before Mrs Ardayre went on to Dorchester, she asked Amaryllis if she had any message to send Denzil: she wanted to watch her face.

It flushed slightly, and her deep soft voice said a little eagerly:

"Yes, tell him I have been so delighted to meet you, and you are just what he said I should find you; and tell him I send him all sorts of good wishes. . . ."

Then she became a little confused.

"I should so love a photograph of you. Would you give me one, I wonder?" the elder woman asked quickly, to avoid any pause, and while Amaryllis went out of the room to get it, she thought:

'She is certainly in love with Denzil. It could not have been the first time he had seen her, at the dinner, and yet he never tells lies.'

And she grew more and more puzzled and interested.

When Amaryllis was alone after the motor with Mrs Ardayre in it had departed, an uncontrollable fit of restlessness came over her.

The visit had stirred up all her emotions again, and she could not grieve any more about the tragedy of John.

Her whole being was vibrating with thoughts of Denzil and desire for his presence; she could see his face and feel the joy of his kisses.

At that moment she would have flung away everything in life to rush into his arms!

Chapter
Seven

Denzil was wounded at Neuve-Chapelle on March 10, 1915, though not seriously, a flesh wound in the side. He had done most gallantly and was to get a D.S.O.

He had been in the hospital for two weeks, and was almost well when Amaryllis came up to Brook Street on April 1.

She had read his name in the list of wounded, and had telegraphed to his mother in great anxiety, but had been reassured, and now she throbbed with longing to see him.

To know that soon he would be going back to the Front was almost more than she could bear.

She was feeling wonderfully well in herself. Her splendid constitution and youth made natural things cause her little distress. And she looked very beautiful with her added dignity of mien and perfectly chosen clothes.

Mrs Ardayre came at once to see her the morning after her arrival, and suggested that Denzil should come when out driving that afternoon.

Amaryllis tried to accept this suggestion calmly, and not show her joy, and Mrs Ardayre left, promising to bring her son about four o'clock.

"Mother, I want to see Amaryllis," Denzil had said, when he knew that Amaryllis was coming to London. "Please arrange it for me, and, Mother, don't ask me anything about it; just leave me there when we arrive, and come and fetch me when I must go again."

So his mother had obediently arranged matters, and at about four in the afternoon left him at the Brook Street door.

Early as it was, Amaryllis had made the tea, and expected to see both Denzil and his mother.

The room was full of hyacinths and daffodils, and she herself looked like a spring flower as she sat on the sofa among the green silk cushions, wrapped in a pale parma-violet tea-gown.

The butler announced, "Captain Ardayre," and Denzil came in slowly, and murmured, "How do you do?"

But as soon as the door was closed upon him he started forward, forgetting his stiff side.

He covered her hands with kisses, for he could not contain his joy; and then he drew back and looked at her with worship and reverence in his blue eyes.

The most mysterious, quivering emotions were coursing through him, mixed with triumph, as he took in the picture she made.

This delicate, beautiful creature! And to see her—so!

Amaryllis lowered her head in sweet confusion; her feelings were no less aroused. She was thrilling with passionate welcome and delicious shyness.

Nature was indeed ruling them both, and with a glad "Darling angel!" Denzil sat down beside her and clasped her in his arms.

Then for a few seconds delirious pleasure was all that they knew.

"Let me look at you again, sweetheart," he ordered presently, with a tone of command and possession in his very deep voice, which caused Amaryllis delight.

It made her feel that she really belonged to him.

"To me you have never been so beautiful, and every scrap of you is mine!"

"Absolutely yours."

"I had to come; I cannot help whether it is right or wrong. I must get back to the Front as soon as I am fit, and I could not have borne to go without seeing you, darling one."

They had a hundred things to say to each other about themselves and about the baby, and the next hour was very sacred and wonderful. Denzil was a superlatively perfect lover and knew the immense value of tender words.

He intoxicated Amaryllis's imagination with the moving things he said.

He spoke of the child and what it meant to him that it should be his and hers. He caused her to feel that he was strong and protective, and that she was to be cherished and adored.

He made pictures of how it would be if he could spend a whole day and night with her presently in June, when she would be quite well, and of how thrilled with interest he would be to see the baby, and that of course it must be exactly like himself!

And Amaryllis's eyes, all soft and swimming with emotion, answered him.

Naturally, since she loved him so passionately, the child would be in his image!

They spent another hour of divine intoxication, and then the clock struck six.

Amaryllis gave a little cry.

"Denzil, it is altogether unnatural that you should have to go. To think that you must leave me, and may not even welcome your son!"

"Darling—darling!" And Denzil fiercely kissed her, he was so deeply moved.

"Heart of me, I must have some news of you. My mother is really trustworthy: will you let her be with you as often as you can, that she may be able to tell me how you are, precious one?

"When the seventh of May comes, I shall go perfectly mad with suspense and anxiety. I will arrange that my mother sends me a telegram at once."

"Denzil!"

And Amaryllis clung to him.

"It is an impossible situation," he said, and he gave a great sigh.

"I shall tell John that I have seen you. I cannot help it, the times are too precarious to have acted otherwise. And afterwards, when the war is over, we must face the matter and decide what is to be done."

"I cannot live without you, Denzil, and that I know."

They said good-bye at last, silently, after many kisses and tears, and Denzil came out into the darkening street to his mother in the motor, with a white, set face.

"I am a little troubled, dearest boy," she whispered as they went along. "I feel that there is something underneath all this, and that Amaryllis means some great thing in your life.

"The whole aspect of everything fills me with

discomfort. It is unlike your usual, sensitive refinement, Denzil, to have gone to see her now. . . ."

"I understand exactly what you mean, Mother. I should say the same thing myself in your place. I can't explain anything, only I beg of you to trust me. Amaryllis is an angel of purity and sweetness; perhaps someday you will understand."

She took his hand into her muff and held it.

Before they reached the hospital door in Park Lane, Mrs Ardayre had been instructed to send an immediate telegram the moment the baby was born, and to comfort and take care of Amaryllis, and tell her son every little detail as to her welfare and the child's.

"I will try not to form any opinion, Denzil, and someday perhaps things will be made plain, for it would break my heart to believe that you are a dishonourable man."

"You need not worry, Mother dearest. Indeed I am not that. It is just a tragic story, but I cannot say any more. Only take care of Amaryllis, and send me news as often as you can."

*   *   *

The telegram to say that Amaryllis had had a little son came to John Ardayre on the night before he went into the trenches again at the second battle of Ypres on May 9, 1915.

He had been waiting in feverish impatience and expectancy all the day, and in fact for three days, for news.

Denzil was just back now and in the trenches again with the rest of the dismounted cavalry. They might meet in the attack at dawn.

When John read the telegram from his aunt, Lady de la Paule, his emotion was so great that he staggered a little, and a friend standing by in the billet took out his flask and gave him some brandy.

Then it seemed as though he went mad.

The Ardayres were saved! The family would carry on!

Fondest love for Amaryllis welled up in his heart.

If he only came through, he would devote his life to showing her his gratitude and showering everything upon her which her heart could desire; and perhaps, perhaps the joy of the baby would make up for the absence of Denzil.

This thought stayed with him and comforted him.

Lady de la Paule had wired:

A splendid little son born 11:45 A.M., *May 7. Amaryllis well, all love.*

And an hour or two before this, Denzil had also received the news from his mother. He too had grown exalted and thanked God.

So dawned the day that the Germans were to fail at Ypres and destiny was to accomplish itself for these two men.

*   *   *

Of what use to write of that terrible fight and of the gas and the horror and the mud?

John Ardayre seemed to bear a charmed life as he led his men "over the top."

For an hour, with exaltation and gladness, he rallied them and cheered them on.

When John had rushed forward to succour a wounded trooper, a shell crashed near them, and he fell to the ground.

And then he knew what the great thing was

that the New Year had promised him. For death was going to straighten out matters; John was going Beyond.

Well, he had never been rebellious, and he knew now that light had come.

The sky above him seemed to be darkening curiously, and the terrible noise to be growing dim, when he was conscious that a man was crawling towards him, dragging a leg, and then his eyes opened wildly for an instant, and he saw that it was Denzil, all covered with blood.

"Are we both going West, Denzil?" he demanded faintly. "At least I am."

Then he gasped a little, while a stream of scarlet flowed from his shattered side.

"I've asked you in a letter to marry Amaryllis immediately, if you get home. I hope your number is not up too, because she will be all alone. Take care of her, Denzil, and take care of the child. . . ."

His voice grew lower and lower, and the last words came in spasms.

"There is an Ardayre son, you know, so it's all right. The family is saved from Ferdinand, and I am very glad to die."

Denzil tried to get out his flask, but before he could reach John's lips with it he saw that it would be of no avail. For death had claimed the head of the family.

And above his mangled body John's face wore a look of calm serenity, and his firm lips smiled.

Then things became all vague for Denzil, and he remembered nothing more.

*   *   *

It was more than two months before Denzil was well enough to be brought from Boulogne, and then he had a relapse, and for the whole of July was dangerously ill.

At one moment there seemed to be no hope of saving his leg, and his mother ate her heart out with anxiety.

And Amaryllis, back at Ardayre with little Benedict, wept many tears.

John's death had deeply grieved her. She realised his steadfast kindness and affection for her.

He had written her a letter just before the battle had begun, a short epistle telling her calmly that the chances would be perhaps even for any man to come out of it alive, and assuring her of his greatest devotion.

"I know that Denzil went to see you, my dear little girl," he had written. "He has told me about it. And I know that you love each other. There is only one chance for us in the future, and that lies with the child. You were an innocent factor in all this, and it would be unjust that you should be hurt."

How good and generous John had always been.

And his letter to his lawyers! To make things smooth for her, and for Denzil—how marvellously kind!

Her mourning for John was real and deep, as it would have been for a brother.

But during the month of intense anxiety about Denzil, everything else was numbed, even her interest in her son.

By the end of August he was out of danger, although little hope was entertained that he would ever walk easily.

But this was a minor thing, and gradually it began to be some consolation to the two women who loved him, to know that he was safely wounded and would probably not be fit for active service again for a very long time.

They wrote letters to each other, but they decided not to meet. Six months must elapse at least, they both felt, even in spite of John's commands.

Another shell must have dropped where John had fallen, for his body was never found, only his field-glasses, broken and battered.

And there would have been no actual information about his death, had not Denzil seen him die.

*   *   *

Harietta Boleski and Stanislass and Ferdinand Ardayre had remained in Paris, with visits to Fontainbleau.

When John had been killed, Harietta had been extremely perturbed.

"Now Stépan will be able to marry that odious bit of bread and butter, and he is sure to do it, after the year!"

This thought rankled her and embittered towards everything. Nothing pleased her. She grew more than ever rebellious at the dullness in which she had to live.

And so the months went by and November came, and in Harietta a madness of jealousy for Amaryllis Ardayre was gradually augmenting.

Verischenzko had gone to Russia in September, and she was convinced that he loved Amaryllis and that the child was his.

She could not conceive of a spiritual devotion; and besides, something had altered all Stépan's way.

From the moment he had returned to Paris until he had left, she had tried and been unable to invoke any response in him, and she had felt like a foiled tigress when another has eaten her prey.

An incident late in November caused her jealousy to burst into flame.

She heard that Verischenzko had returned from Russia, and she went to his rooms to see him. The Russian servant who was accustomed to receive her was there waiting for his master, who had not yet arrived.

Without a word she passed the old man when he opened the door, and made her way into the sitting-room, and then into the bedroom beyond.

She did not believe that Stépan was not there, and wanted to make sure. It was empty, but a light burned before an ikon, the doors of which were closed.

Curiosity made Harietta go close and examine it. She knew the room so well, and had never seen it there before.

The table beneath it was arranged like an altar, and the ikon was let into the carved *boiserie* of the wall. It must have been since he had parted with her that this ridiculous thing had been done!

She had not entered his *appartement* since June. She felt angry that the shrine should be closed and that she could not look upon it, for it must certainly be something which Verischenzko prized.

She bent nearer and shook the little doors; they resisted her, and her temper rose. Then some force seemed to propel her to commit sacrilege.

She shook and shook and tore at the golden clasp, her irritation giving strength and cunning to her hands; and at last the small bolt came undone and the doors flew open.

An exquisitely painted modern picture of the Virgin was disclosed holding the Christ-Child in her arms.

But for all the saintliness in the eyes of Mary,

the face was an exact portrait of Amaryllis Ardayre!

Nothing had ever moved her so forcibly.

She took out her pearl hatpin and stabbed out the eyes of the Virgin, almost shaking with passion, and scratched and obliterated the face of the Christ-Child.

This done, she extinguished the little lamp and slammed the doors.

She laughed savagely as she went back into the sitting-room.

"The Virgin indeed, and *his* child. Well, I've taught him!"

And she flung past the Russian servant with a look which was a curse, so that the old man crossed himself and quickly barred the entrance door, when she stamped off down the stairs.

Arriving in her gilded salon at the Universal, she felt she would like to wring someone's neck. She had never been so full of rage in her life.

She did find a little satisfaction in a kick at Fou-Chou, who fled, whining, to his faithful Marie, who had come in to carry away her mistress's sable cloak.

The maid's face became thunderous. A look of sullen hate gleamed in her dark eyes.

"She will kick you, my angel, just once too often," she murmured to the wee creature when she had carried him from the room. "And then we shall see. Your Marie knows that which may punish her someday soon!"

Harietta, quite indifferent to these matters, telephoned immediately to Ferdinand Ardayre.

He must come to her instantly, without a moment's delay.

A plan which might give her some satisfaction to execute had evolved itself in her brain.

He was in his room in another part of the building, and hastened to obey her command. She was livid with anger and seemed to have grown old.

She went over and kissed him voluptuously, and then she whispered hoarsely:

"Ferdie, now you have got to do something for me. You are not going to let the child of Verischenzko be master of Ardayre. We are going to gain time, and perhaps someday be able to do away with it. Now I have got a plan which will lighten your heart."

She knew that she could count upon him, for since the birth of the little Benedict and the death of John, Ferdinand had stormed with threats of vengeance, while knowing his impotency.

His life with Harietta had grown a torment and a hell, but with every fresh unkindness and pang of jealousy she caused him, his low passion for her increased.

He knew that she loved Verischenzko, whom he hated with all his might, and if she now proposed to hurt both his enemies, he would assist her joyfully.

"Tell me," he begged.

So she drew him to the sofa and picked up a block and pencil.

"Do you possess any of the writing of your dead brother, John, or if you don't, can you get some from anywhere?"

Ferdinand's face blazed with excitement. What was she going to suggest?

"I always keep one letter, in which he ordered me never to address him, and told me I was not of his blood, but was a mongrel Turk."

"That is splendid. Where is it? Have you got it here?"

"Yes, in my despatch-box. I'll go and fetch it now."

"Very well. I will get rid of Stanislass for the evening and we can have some hours alone; and you will see if I don't help to worry them hideously, Ferdie, even if that is all we can do."

And when he had left her presence she paced the room excitedly.

"It will prevent Stépan's marrying her at all events for a long time," she told herself.

The thought that she had lost Verischenzko completely unbalanced her. It was the first time in her life that she had had to relinquish a man. And she hated to have to realise how highly he must hold Amaryllis.

He seemed the only thing she wanted now in life, and she knew that he was quite beyond her, and that indeed he had never been hers. The one human being whom she had attracted and yet never been able to intoxicate and draw against his will.

She would have torn the flesh from Amaryllis's face, had she been there, and thrust her hatpin into her real eyes.

But the spoke should be put in the wheel of Verischenzko's marrying her! And perhaps some other revenge would come.

Hans? Hans should be made to carry the scheme through, Hans and Ferdinand.

She dug her nails into the palms of her hands. No wild animal in its cage could have felt more rage.

Then when Ferdinand returned with John's letter, she controlled herself and sat down at the table beside him, and supervised his attempts at copying the writing, while she unfolded the details of her scheme.

"You know John's body was never found," she informed him presently. "I heard all the details from a man who was there; they only picked up his glasses and his boot.

He could very well have been taken prisoner by the Germans and be in the hospital there, too ill to have written for all this time.

"Now, think how he ought to word his first letter to his precious bread-and-butter wife!"

"There must only be the fewest words, because I don't know what terms they were on. I think a post-card, if we could get one, would be the best thing."

"Of course. I have someone who can see to that. It will be worth waiting the week for. I will procure several, and meanwhile you must practise his hand."

At the end of half-an-hour a very creditable forgery had been secured, and the two jealous beings felt satisfied with their work for the time.

*   *   *

It had been arranged that Denzil and his mother should spend Christmas with Amaryllis at Ardayre. Both felt that it was going to be the most wonderful moment when they should meet.

There were no obstacles now to their happiness, and everything promised to be full of joy. The months which had gone by since John's death had been turning Amaryllis into a more serene and forceful being.

The whole burden of the estate had fallen upon her young shoulders, and she had endeavoured to carry it with dignity and success, and yet have time to spare for her war organisations in the county.

She had developed extraordinarily, and had grown from a very pretty girl into a most beautiful young woman.

What would Denzil think of her? That was her preoccupation. And what would he think of the baby Benedict?

Her guests were to be there on December 23, and when the hour came for the motor to arrive from the station, Amaryllis grew hot and cold with excitement.

She had made herself look quite exquisite in a soft black frock, and her heart was beating almost to suffocation when she heard the footsteps in the hall.

Then the green drawing-room door opened and Colonel and Mrs Ardayre were announced, and were immediately greeted by the great tawny dogs and then by their mistress.

A pang contracted her heart when she caught sight of Denzil. He was so very pale and thin, and he walked painfully and slowly with a stick.

He was only a wreck of the splendid lover who had come to Ardayre before. But he was always Denzil of the ardent eyes and the crisp bronze-coloured hair.

Her attraction for Denzil had increased a hundredfold. He thought, as she sat there pouring out the tea, of how he would woo her with subtlety before he would claim her for his own.

He was stimulated by her sweet shyness and her tender aloofness.

The tea seemed to him to be interminably long, and he wished for it to end.

Mrs Ardayre behaved with admirable tact. She spoke of all sorts of light and friendly things, and then asked about the baby. Was he not wonderful now, at seven months old!

The lovely, vivid pink deepened in Amaryllis's smooth velvety cheeks, and her grey eyes became as soft as a doe's.

"You shall see him in the morning. He will be asleep now. Of course to me he is wonderful, but I dare say he is only an ordinary child."

She had peeped at Denzil and had seen that his face fell a little as she said they should only see the baby the next day, and she had felt a wave of joy.

She knew that she meant to take him up quietly presently, just he and she alone!

After they had finished tea, Mrs Ardayre suggested that she should go to her room.

"I am tired, Amaryllis dear," she announced cheerily, "and I shall rest for an hour before dinner."

"Come then, and I will show you both your rooms."

They came up the broad staircase with her, Denzil a step at a time, slowly, and at the top she stopped and said to him:

"Perhaps you will remember that is the door of the cedar parlour at the end of the passage. You will find me there when I have installed your mother comfortably. Your room is next to hers."

Some contrary nervousness made her remain for quite a little while.

Was Cousin Beatrice sure that she was comfortable? Had she everything she wanted? Her maid was already unpacking, and all was warm, and fresh-scented with lavender, and bowls of violets on the dressing-table.

"My dear child, it is Paradise, and you are a perfect angel. I shall revel in it after the cold journey down."

So at last there was no excuse to stay longer, and Amaryllis left the room; but in the passage it seemed as though her knees were trembling, and as she passed the top of the staircase she leaned for a second or two on the balustrade.

The longed-for moment had come!

When she opened the door of the cedar parlour, with its soft lamps and great glowing logs, she saw that Denzil was already there, seated on the sofa beside the fire.

She ran to him before he could rise: the movement, she knew, would be pain to him. And then she sank down beside him and held out her hands.

"Beloved darling!" he whispered in exultation, and she slipped forward into his arms.

Oh, the bliss of it all! After the months of separation, and the horrible trenches and the battles and the suffering, the days and nights of agonising pain!

It seemed to Denzil that his being melted within him. Heaven itself had come.

They could not speak coherently for some moments, for everything was too filled with holy joy.

"At last, at last!" he cried presently. "Now we shall part no more!"

Then he had to be assured that she loved him still.

"It is I who must take care of you now, Denzil, and I shall love to do that," she cooed.

"I have not thought much of the hurt," he answered her. "For all these months I have just been living for this day, and now it has come, darling one, and I can hardly believe that it is true, it is so absolutely divine."

They could not talk of anything but themselves and love for an hour. They told each other of their longings and anxieties, and at last they spoke of John.

"He was so splendid," Denzil said, "unselfish to the very end."

He then described to Amaryllis how he actually had died, and told of his last words, and their thought for her.

"If he could see us, I think he would be glad that we are happy."

"I know that he would."

But the tears had gathered in her eyes.

Denzil stroked her hand gently. He did not make any lover's caress, and she appreciated his understanding, and after a little she leaned against his arm.

"Denzil, when we live here together, we must always try to carry out all that John would have wished to do; it meant his very soul. And you will help me to be a worthy mother of the Ardayre son."

She had not spoken of the child before; some unaccountable shyness had restrained her, even in their fondest moments.

And yet the thought had never been absent from either. It had throbbed there in their hearts. It was going to be so exquisite to whisper about it presently.

And Denzil had waited until she mentioned this dear interest. He did not wish to assume any rights or take anything for granted.

She should be queen, not only of his heart but of everything, until she should herself accord him authority.

But his eyes grew fitful now as he leaned nearer to her.

"Darling, am I not going to be allowed to see my son?"

Then, with a cry, Amaryllis bent forward and was clasped in his arms. All her wayward shyness

melted, and she poured forth her delight in the
baby, their very own.

"You will see that he is just you, Denzil, as we
knew that he would be; and now I will go and
fetch him for you and bring him here, because the
stairs up to the nursery are so steep they might
hurt you to climb."

She left him swiftly, and was not long gone,
and Denzil sat there by the fire trembling with an
emotion which he could not have described in words.

The door opened again and Amaryllis returned with the tiny sleeping form, in its long white
nightgown and wrapped in a great fleecy shawl.

She crept up to him very softly; the little one
was sound asleep. She made a sign to Denzil not to
rise, and she bent down and placed the bundle
tenderly in his arms.

Then they gazed at the little face together
with worshipping eyes.

He was just a round, pink-and-white cherub,
like thousands of others in the world, with very
long eyelashes, sweeping his sleep-flushed cheeks,
and minute rings of bronze-gold hair curling over
the edge of his close cambric cap.

But he seemed to those two looking at him to
be unique, and more beautiful than the dawn.

"Isn't he perfect, Denzil?" whispered Amaryllis in ecstasy.

"Marvellous!" Denzil's voice was awed.

Then the wonder and the divinity of love and
its spirit of creation came over them both and a
mist of deep feeling grew in their eyes.

*   *   *

At dinner they were all so happy together.

Mrs Ardayre was a note of harmony anywhere.

She had gradually grown to understand the situation in the months of her son's recovering from his wounds, and although no actual words had passed between them, Denzil felt that his mother had divined the truth, and it made things easier.

Afterwards, in the green drawing-room, Amaryllis played to them and delighted their ears, and then they went up to the cedar parlour and sat round the fire and talked and made plans.

If it should be quite hopeless that Denzil could ever return to the Front, or be of service behind the lines, he meant to enter Parliament.

The thought that his active soldiering was probably done was very bitter to him, and the two women who loved him tried to create an enthusiasm for the Parliamentary idea.

The one certainty was that his adventurous spirit would never remain behind in the background, whatever occurred.

They would be married at the beginning of February, they decided. The whole of their world knew of John's written wishes, and no unkind comments would be likely to arise.

And when Beatrice Ardayre left them alone to say good-night to each other, Denzil drew Amaryllis back to his side.

"I think the world is going to be a totally new place, darling, after the war. If it goes on very long, the gradual privation and suffering and misery will create a new order of things, and all of us should be ready to face it.

"You will advance with me, sweetheart, will you not, even if it should seem to be a chasm we are crossing?"

"Denzil, of course I will."

He sighed a little.

"Stépan will be arriving in London next week.

I heard from him today. Won't you ask him down, darling, to spend the New Year with us here? It would be so good to see him again."

This was agreed upon, and then they drifted back to lover's whisperings, and presently they said a fond good-night.

*   *   *

Christmas Day of 1915 and the week which followed were like some happy dream for Denzil and Amaryllis. Each hour seemed to discover some new aspect which caused further understanding and love to augment.

They spent long afternoons in the cedar parlour, dipping into books, and a delicious pleasure was for Amaryllis to be nestled in Denzil's arms on the sofa while he read aloud to her in his deep, magnetic voice.

Beatrice Ardayre at this period was like a pleased mother-cat purring in the sun while her kittens gamboled. Her well beloved was content, and she was satisfied.

She always seemed to be there when wanted and yet to leave the lovers principally to themselves.

Verischenzko was to arrive in time for dinner on the last day of the old year.

That afternoon was one of even unusually perfect happiness, motoring slowly round the park and up onto the hills in Amaryllis's little two-seater, which she drove herself.

They got out at the top and leaned upon a gate from which they seemed to be looking down over the world.

Peaceful, smiling, prosperous England!

Miles and miles of her fairest country lay there in front of them, giving no echo of war.

Denzil put an arm round her and drew her close to him and clasped her fondly.

"Just for a little we must try to forget about the war. I never dreamed of such perfect happiness as we are having, sweetheart, my own."

"Nor I, Denzil. I am almost afraid. . . ."

But he kissed her passionately and bade this thought be gone.

Afraid of what? Nothing mattered since they would always be together. February would soon come, and then they would never part again.

So the vague foreboding passed from Amaryllis's heart, and in fond visionings they whispered plans for the spring and the summer and the growing years.

And so at last they returned to the house and found the afternoon post waiting for them. Filson had just brought it in, and Amaryllis's letters lay in a pile on her writing-table.

There happened to be none for Denzil, and he went over to the fireplace, and was stroking the head of Mercury, the greatest of the big tawny dogs, when he was startled by an ominous little cry from his beloved.

On looking up, he saw that she had sunk into a chair, her face deadly pale, while there had fluttered to the floor at her feet a torn envelope and a foreign-looking post-card.

What could this mean?

Chapter Eight

Verischenzko had come straight through from Petrograd to England. He had been delayed and had never returned to Paris since September.

He knew nothing of Harietta's sacrilege as yet. But he had at last accumulated sufficient proof against her to have her entirely in his hands.

He thought over the whole matter as he came down in the train to Ardayre. She was a grave danger to the Allies, and had betrayed them again and again.

He must have no mercy. Her last crimes had been against France; her punishment would be easier to manage there.

The strain of cruelty in his nature came uppermost as he reviewed the evil which she had done.

Stanislass's haunted face seemed to look at him out of the mist of the half-lit carriage. What Poland might have accomplished with such a leader as Boleski had been before this baneful passion fell upon him!

Then he conjured up the imagined faces of the brave Frenchmen who had been betrayed by Harietta to Hans, and shot in Germany.

A spy's death in war-time was not an ignoble one, and they had gone there with their lives in their hands; and had Harietta been true to that side, and had she been acting from patriotism, he could have desired to save her the death sentence now.

But she had never been true, no country mattered to her; she had given to him secrets as well as to Hans.

Then he laughed to himself grimly. So her *danseur* at the Ardayre Ball was the first husband! The man who used to beat her with a stick, and who had let her divorce him in obedience to the Higher Command.

How clever the whole thing was!

If it had not all been so serious, it would have been interesting to allow her to live longer, to watch what next she would do; but the issues at stake were too vital to delay.

He would not hesitate; he would denounce her to the French authorities immediately on his return to Paris, and without one qualm or regret.

She had lived well and played "crooked," and now it was meet that she should pay the price.

Filson announced him in the green drawing-room when he reached Ardayre, but only Denzil rose to greet him, and wrung his hand.

He noticed that his friend's face looked stern and rather pale.

"I'm so awfully glad that you have come, Stépan."

And they exchanged handshakes and greetings.

"You are about the only person I should want to see just now, because you know the whole history. Something unprecedented has happened:

"A communication has come apparently from John to Amaryllis from a prisoners' camp in Germany, and yet, as far as one can be certain of anything, I am certain that I saw him die."

Verischenzko was greatly startled. What a frightful complication it would make should John be alive!

"The letter, merely a post-card enclosed in an envelope, came by this afternoon's post, and as you can understand it has frightfully upset us all. It is a sort of thing about which one cannot analyse one's feelings.

"John has a right to his life and we ought to be glad, but the idea of giving up Amaryllis, of having all the suffering and the parting again, Stépan—it is cruelly hard."

Verischenzko sat down in one of the big green chairs.

"John wrote to her himself, you say? It is not a message through a third person—no?"

"It appears to be in his own writing."

Denzil stood leaning on the mantelpiece, and his face seemed to grow more haggard with each word.

"Merely saying that he was taken prisoner by the enemy when they made the counter-attack, and that he has been too ill to write or speak until now."

He paused, his voice sounding puzzled.

"I can't understand it, because they did not make the counter-attack until after I was carried in, and even though I was unconscious then, the stretcher-bearers must have seen John when they lifted me, if he had been there.

"Nothing was found but his glasses, and we concluded that another shell had burst somewhere near his body after I was carried in.

"Stépan, I swear to God I saw him die."

"It sounds extraordinary. Try to tell me every detail, Denzil."

So the story of John's last moments was gone over again, and all the most minute events which had occurred.

Verischenzko was silent for a moment, then he asked:

"May I see my lady Amaryllis?'"

"Yes, she told me to bring you to her as soon as I should have explained to you the whole affair. Come now."

They went up the stairs together, and they hardly spoke a word, and when they reached the cedar parlour Denzil let Verischenzko go in in front of him.

"I have brought Stépan to you," he told Amaryllis. "I am going to leave you to talk now."

Amaryllis was white as milk and her grey eyes were disturbed and very troubled. She held out her two hands to Verischenzko, and he kissed them with affectionate worship.

"Lady of My Soul!"

"Oh, Stépan, comfort me, give me counsel. It is such a terrible moment in my life. What am I to do?"

"It is indeed difficult for you. We must think it all out."

"Poor John, I ought to be glad that he is alive, and I am, really . . . only, oh, Stépan, I love Denzil so dearly. It is all too awfully complicated.

"What so greatly astonishes me about it is that John has not written deliriously, or as though he has lost his memory, and yet if we had carried out his instructions and wishes we should be married now, Denzil and I, and he never alludes to the possibility of this! It is written as though no complications could enter into the case."

"It sounds strange. May I see the letter?"

She got up and went over to the writing-table,

and returned with a packet and the envelope which contained the card.

It was not one which prisoners use as a rule; it had the picture of a German town on it, and the post-mark on the envelope was of a place in Holland.

Verischenzko read it carefully.

> *I have been too ill to write before. I was taken prisoner in the counter-attack and was unconscious. I am sending this by the kindness of a nurse through Holland.*
>
> *Everyone must have believed that I was dead. I am longing for news of you, dearest. I shall soon be well. Do not worry. I am going to be moved and will write again with address. All love,*
>
> *John*

The writing was rather feeble, as a very ill person's would naturally be, but the name "John" was firm and very legible.

"You are certain that it is his writing?"

"Yes!"

She handed him another letter from the packet, John's last one to her.

"You can see for yourself it is the same hand."

Stépan took both over to the lamp, and was bending to examine them when he gave a little cry:

"*Sapristi!*"

And instead of looking at the writings, he sniffed strongly at the card, and then again.

Amaryllis watched him, amazed.

"The same! By the Lord, it is the work of Ferdinand. No one could mistake his scent who had once smelt it. The musk rot, the scorpion!

"But he has betrayed himself."

Amaryllis grew paler as she came close beside him.

"Stépan, oh, tell me . . . what do you mean?"

"I believe this to be a forgery; the scent is a clue to me. Smell it. There is a lingering sickly aroma round it. It came in an envelope, you see, and that would preserve it. It is an Eastern perfume, very heavy. What do you say?"

She wrinkled her delicate nose.

"Yes, there is some scent from it. One perceives it at first and then it goes off. Oh, Stépan, please do not torture me. Can you be quite sure?"

"I am absolutely certain that whether it is in John's writing or not, Ferdinand, or someone who uses his unique scent, has touched that card. Now we must investigate everything."

He walked up and down the room in agitation for a few moments, talking rapidly to himself, half in Russian.

Amaryllis caught bits:

"Ferdinand, how to his advantage? None. What then? Harietta? Harietta, but why for her? . . ."

Then he sat down and stared into the fire, his yellow-green eyes blazing with intelligence, his clear brain balancing up things. But now he did not speak his thoughts aloud.

'She is jealous. I remember she imagined that it is my child. She believes I may marry Amaryllis. It is as plain as day!'

He jumped up and excitedly held out his hands.

"Let us fetch Denzil!" he cried joyously. "I can explain everything."

Denzil when he came into the room looked from one face to the other anxiously, and Stépan immediately spoke.

"I think that the card is a forgery, Denzil. I believe it to have been written by Ferdinand Ardayre, at the instigation of Harietta Boleski. She would have means to obtain the post-card and have it sent through Holland too."

"But why, why should she?" Amaryllis asked in wonderment. "What possible reason could she have for wishing to be so cruel to us? We were always very nice to her, as you know."

"She was jealous of you all the same!" Verischenzko laughed cynically. "But, Denzil, I track it by the scent. I know Ferdinand uses that scent."

He held out the card.

"Smell."

Denzil sniffed as Amaryllis had done.

"It is so faint I should not have remarked it unless you had told me; but I dare say if it was a scent one had smelt before one would be struck by it! But how are you going to prove it, Stépan?

"We shall have to have convincing proof, because I am the only witness of poor John's death, and it could easily be said that I am too deeply interested to be reliable.

"For God's sake, old friend, think of some way of making a certainty."

"I have a way which I can enforce as soon as I reach Paris. Meanwhile, say nothing to anyone, and put the thought of it out of your heads."

Amaryllis's lips were trembling; the shock and then the counter-shock were unhinging her.

She was horrified at herself that she should not catch at every straw to prove John was alive, instead of feeling some sense of relief when Verischenzko protested that the post-card was a forgery.

But she knew that had she the choice she would rather be dead than separated now from Denzil. And if John were really to be alive, what misery he would be obliged to suffer, knowing the situation.

"Quite apart from what to me is a convincing proof, the scent," Verischenzko went on, "the card must be a forgery because of John's seeming oblivion of the possibility that you two might have already carried out his wishes. All this would have been very unlike him.

"But if it is, as I think, Ferdinand's and Harietta Boleski's work, they would not be likely to know that John had desired that Denzil should marry you, Amaryllis, and so would have thought a short card with longings to see you would be a natural thing to write.

"Indeed, you can be at rest. And now I will go and dress for dinner, and we will forget disturbing thoughts."

*   *   *

When Verischenzko reached Paris and discovered the desecration of the ikon, an icy rage came over him.

He knew, even before questioning his old servant, that it could only be the work of Harietta. Jealousy alone would be the cause of such a wanton act.

It revealed to him the certainty of his theory that she had imagined the little Benedict to be his child.

No further proof that the post-card was a forgery was really needed, but he would see her once more and obtain extra confirmation.

His yellow-green eyes gleamed in a curious way as he stood looking at the mutilated picture.

That her ridiculous and accursed hatpin should have dared to touch the eyes of the Lady of His Soul, and scratch out the face of the child!

But he must not let this emotion of personal anger affect what he intended to do in any case, from motives of justice.

In the morning he would give all his proofs of her guilt to the French authorities, and let the law take its course, but tonight he would make her come there to his apartment and hear from him an indictment of her crimes.

After half-an-hour had gone by, he rose and went to the telephone. He called up the Universal and asked to be put through to the apartment of *Madame* Boleski, and soon heard Harietta's voice.

It was a little anxious, and yet insolent too.

"Yes? Is that you? Stépan! Darling brute! What do you want?"

"You. Cannot you come and dine with me tonight, alone?"

His voice was honey-sweet, with a spontaneous, frank ring in it; only his face still looked as a fiend's.

"You have just arrived? How divine!"

"This instant, so I rushed at once to the telephone. I—long for you. Come—now."

He allowed passion to quiver in the last notes. He must be sure that she would be drawn.

'He cannot have opened the doors of the ikon,' Harietta thought. 'I will go. To see him again will be worth it, anyway!'

"All right, in half-an-hour."

Then he went again to the ikon and examined the doors. By slamming them very hard and readjusting one small golden nail, he could give the fastening the appearance of its having been jammed and impossible to open.

He ordered a wonderful dinner and some Château Yquem of 1900.

Harietta arrived punctually. She had made herself extremely beautiful. Her overmastering desire to see Verischenzko had allowed her usually keen sense of self-preservation partially to sleep.

But even so, underneath there was some undefined sense of uneasiness.

Stépan met her in the hall, and greeted her in his usual abrupt way, without ceremony.

"You will leave your cloak in my room," he suggested, wishing to give her the chance to look at the ikon's jammed doors and so put her at her ease.

The moment she found herself alone, she went swiftly to the shrine. She examined it closely; no, the bolt had not been mended. She pulled at the doors, but she could not open them, and she remembered with relief that she had slammed them hard.

That would account for things. He certainly could not yet know of her action. The evening would be one of pleasure after all. And there was never any use in speculating about tomorrows.

Verischenzko was waiting for her in the sitting-room, and they went straight in to dinner. A little table was drawn up to the fire; all appeared deliciously intimate, and Harietta's spirits rose.

Her eyes swam with passion as she leaned over the table, whispering words of the most violent love in his ears.

Verischenzko remained absolutely unstirred.

"How silly you were to send that post-card to Lady Ardayre," he remarked contemplatively in the middle of one of her burning sentences.

"It was not worthy of your usual methods: a child could see that it was a forgery. If you had not done that I might have made you very happy tonight, for the last time, my little goat!"

"Stépan . . . what card? But you are going to make me happy anyway, darling brute! That is what I have come for, and you know it."

Her eyes were not so successfully innocent as usual when she lied. She was uneasy at his stolidity; some fear stayed with her that perhaps he meant not to gratify her desires just to be provoking.

He had teased her more than once before.

Verischenzko went on, lighting his cigarette calmly:

"It was a silly plot. Ferdinand Ardayre wrote it and you dictated it. I perceived the whole thing at once. You did it because you were jealous of Lady Ardayre; you believe that I love her."

"I do not know anything about a card, but I *am* jealous about that hateful bit of bread and butter!"

Her eyes flashed.

"It is so unlike you to worry over such a creature; I'm what you like!"

He laughed softly.

"A man has many sides. You appeal to his lowest. Fortunately, it is not in command of him all the time.

"But let me tell you more about the forgery. You over-reached yourselves. You made John ignore something which would have been his first thought. Thus, the fraud was exposed at once."

Her jealousy blazed up, so that she forgot herself and her prudence.

"You mean about the child . . . your child . . ."

The ominous gleam came into Verischenzko's eyes.

"My child! You spoke of it once before, and I warned you. I never speak idly."

She got up from the table and came and flung her arms round his neck.

"Stépan, I love you . . . I love you! I would like to kill Amaryllis and the child. I want you. Why are you so changed?"

He only laughed scornfully again while he disengaged her arms.

"Do you know how I found out? By the perfume, the same as you told me must be that of Stanislass's mistress, on the handkerchief marked 'F.A.' The whole thing was dramatically childish. You thought that to prove her husband was still alive would stop my marriage with Amaryllis Ardayre!"

"Then you are going to marry her!"

Harietta's hazel eyes flashed fire; her face had grown distorted with passion and her cheeks burned beyond the rouge.

She appeared a most revolting sight to Stépan. He watched her with cold, critical eyes. As she put out her hands he noticed how the thumbs turned right back.

How had he ever been able to touch her in the past!

He shivered with disgust and degradation at the thought.

She saw his movement of repulsion and completely lost her head.

She flung herself into his arms and almost strangled him in her furious embrace, while she threw all restraint to the winds and poured out a torrent of passion, intermingled with curses for one who had dared to try and rob her of this adored mate.

It was a wonderful and very sickening exhibition, Verischenzko thought.

He remained as a statue of ice.

Then, when she had exhausted herself a little, he spoke with withering calm.

"Control yourself, Harietta. Such emotion will leave ugly lines, and you cannot afford to spoil the one good you possess. I have not the least desire for you; I find that you look plain and only bore me. But now listen to me for a little, I have something to say."

His voice changed from the cynical callousness to a deep note of gravity.

"You need not even tell me in words that you sent the forgery, you have given me ample proof. That subject is finished, but I will make you listen to the recital of some of your vile deeds."

The note grew sterner and his eyes held her cowed.

"Ah, what instruments of the devil are such women as you. Possessing the greatest of all power over men, you have used it only for ill. Wherever you have passed there is a trail of degradation and slime."

She sank to her knees at his side.

He went on mercilessly. He spoke of many names which she knew, and then he came to Ferdinand Ardayre.

"They tell me he is drinking and sodden with morphine, and raves wildly of you. Think of them all, where are they now? Dead, many of them, and you have survived and prospered like a vampire, sucking their blood."

His voice sharpened as he said:

"Do you ever think of a human being but your own degraded self? You would sacrifice your nearest and dearest for a moment's personal gain."

She sobbed hoarsely and held out her hands.

"For all these things you might still have gone

free, Harietta, and fate would punish you in time, but you have committed that great crime for which there can be no mercy:

"You have acted the part of a spy. A wretched spy, not for patriotism but for your own ends, and you have not been faithful to either side.

"Have you not often given me the secrets of your first husband, Hans? Do you care one atom which country wins? Not you. The whole sordid business has had only one aim, some personal gratification."

He paused, and she began to speak, now choking with rage, but he motioned her to be silent.

"Do you think so lightly of the great issues which are shaking the world that you imagine that you can do these things with impunity? I tell you that soon you must pay the price. I am not the only one who knows of your ways."

She got up from the floor now and tossed her head.

Important things had never been realities to her. Her fear left her. What agitated her now was that Stépan, whom she adored, should speak to her in such a tone.

She threw herself into his arms once more, passionately proclaiming her love.

He thrust her from him in shrinking disgust, and the cruel vein in his character was aroused.

"Love! Do not dare to desecrate the name of love. You do not know what it means. I do, and this shall always remain with you as a remembrance. I love Amaryllis Ardayre. She is my ideal of a woman, tender and restrained and true.

"I shall always lay my life at her feet. I love her with a love such beings as you cannot dream of, knowing only the senses and playing only to them. That will be your knowledge always, that I worship and revere this woman, and hold you in supreme contempt."

Harietta writhed and whined on the sofa where she had fallen.

"Go," he went on icily. "I have no further use for you, and my car is waiting below; you may as well avail yourself of it and return to your hotel.

"In the morning the last proof of the interest I have taken in you may be given, but tonight you can sleep."

Harietta cried aloud. She was frightened at last. What did he mean? But even fear was swallowed up in the frantic thought that he had done with her, that he would never any more hold her in his arms.

Her world lay in ruins. He seemed the one and only good. She grovelled on the floor and kissed his feet.

"Master, Master! Keep me near you! I will be your slave!"

But Verischenzko pushed her gently aside with his foot, and took up a cigarette. He lighted it serenely, glancing indifferently at the dishevelled heap of a woman still crouching on the floor.

"Enough of this dramatic nonsense. I advise you to go quietly to bed. You may not sleep so softly on future nights."

Fear overcame her again. What could he mean? She got up and held on to the table, searching his face with burning eyes.

"Why should I not sleep so softly always?" she asked in a thick voice.

"Who knows?" He laughed hoarsely. "Life is a gamble in these days. You must ask your interesting German friend."

She became ghastly white. That there was real danger was beginning to dawn upon her. The rouge stood out like that on the painted face of a clown.

Verischenzko remained completely unmoved. He pressed the bell, and his Russian servant, warned beforehand, brought him in his fur coat and hat, and assisted him to put them on.

"I will take *Madame* to get her cloak," he announced calmly. "Wait here to show us out."

There was nothing for Harietta to do but follow him as he went towards the bedroom door. She was stunned.

He walked over to the ikon, and, slipping a paper-knife under them, opened wide the doors; then he turned to her, and the very life melted within her when she saw his face.

"This is your work," and he pointed to the mutilations, "and for that and many other things, Harietta, you shall at last pay the price. Now come, I will take you back to your lover and your husband. Both will be waiting and longing for your return. Come."

She dropped to the floor and refused to move, so that he was obliged to call in the servant, and together they lifted her, the one holding her up while the other wrapped her in her cloak.

Then, each supporting her, they made their way down the stairs, and placed her in the waiting motor, Verischenzko taking the seat at her side, and so they drove to the Universal.

She should sleep tonight in peace and have time to think over the events of the evening.

But tomorrow he must no longer delay about giving information to the authorities.

She cowered in the motor until they had almost reached the door, then she flung her arms round his neck and kissed him wildly again, sobbing with rage and terror:

"You shall not marry Amaryllis. I will kill you both first."

He smiled in the darkness, and she felt that he was mocking her, and suddenly she turned and bit his arm, her teeth meeting in the cloth of his fur-lined coat.

He shook her off as he would have done a rat.

"Never quite apropos, Harietta! Always a little late. But here we have arrived, and you will not care for your admirers, the *concierge,* and the lift-men to see you in such a state. Put your veil over your face and go quietly to your rooms. I will wish you a very good-night and farewell!"

He got out and stood with mock respect uncovered to assist her, and she was obliged to follow him. The hall-porter and the numerous personnel of the hotel were looking on.

He bowed once more and appeared to kiss her hand:

"Good-bye Harietta! Sleep well."

Then he re-entered the car and was whirled away.

She staggered for a second and then moved forward to the lift.

But as she went in, two tall men who had been waiting stepped forward and joined her, and all three were carried aloft, and as she walked to her salon she saw that they were following her.

"There will be no more kicks for you, my angel!" the maid, peeping from a door, whispered exultingly to Fou-Chou. "Your Marie has saved you at last!"

*   *   *

When Verischenzko again reached his own sitting-room he paced up and down for half-an-hour. He was horribly agitated, and angry with himself for being so.

Finally he sat down and wrote to Denzil:

I have all the needed proofs, my friend. Marry my soul's lady in peace and make her happy. There come some phases in a man's life which require all his will to face. I hope I am no weakling. I return to Russia immediately. Events there will enable me to blot out some disturbing memories.

The end is not yet. Indeed, I feel that my real life is only just beginning.

Ferdinand Ardayre is deeply incriminated with Harietta; it is only a question of a little time and he will be taken too. Then, Denzil, you, in the natural course of events, would have been the head of the family.

You will need all your philosophy never to feel any jar in the situation with your son as the years go on. You will have to look at it all squarely, dear old friend, and know that it is impossible to have interfered with destiny and to have gone scot-free.

Then you will be able to accept the affair with common sense, and prize what you have obtained, without spoiling it with futile regrets.

You have paid most of your screw with wounds and sufferings, and now can expect what happiness the agony of the world can let a man enjoy.

My blessings to you both and to the Ardayre son.

And now adieu for a long time.

He had hardly written the last line when the telephone rang, and the frantic voice of Stanislass, his ancient friend, called to him.

Harietta had been taken away to St Lazare; her maid had denounced her. What could be done?

A great wave of relief swept over Stépan. So he was not to be the instrument of justice after all!

How profoundly he thanked God!

But the irony of the thing shook him.

Harietta would pay with her life for having maltreated a dog!

Truly, the workings of fate were marvellous.

ABOUT THE EDITOR

BARBARA CARTLAND, the world's most famous romantic novelist, who is also an historian, playwright, lecturer, political speaker and television personality, has now written over 200 books. She has also had many historical works published and has written four autobiographies as well as the biographies of her mother and that of her brother Ronald Cartland, who was the first Member of Parliament to be killed in the last war. This book has a preface by Sir Winston Churchill. Barbara Cartland has sold 80 million books over the world, more than half of these in the U.S.A. She broke the world record in 1975 by writing twenty books in a year, and her own record in 1976 with twenty-one. In private life, Barbara Cartland, who is a Dame of the Order of St. John of Jerusalem, has fought for better conditions and salaries for Midwives and Nurses. As President of the Royal College of Midwives (Hertfordshire Branch), she has been invested with the first Badge of Office ever given in Great Britain, which was subscribed to by the Midwives themselves. She has also championed the cause for old people and founded the first Romany Gypsy Camp in the world. Barbara Cartland is deeply interested in Vitamin Therapy and is President of the British National Association for Health.

Barbara Cartland's
Library of Love

The World's Great Stories of Romance Specially Abridged
by Barbara Cartland For Today's Readers.

☐	11487	THE SEQUENCE by Elinor Glyn	$1.50
☐	11468	THE BROAD HIGHWAY by Jeffrey Farnol	$1.50
☐	10927	THE WAY OF AN EAGLE by Ethel M. Dell	$1.50
☐	10926	THE REASON WHY by Elinor Glyn	$1.50
☐	10925	THE HUNDREDTH CHANCE by Ethel M. Dell	$1.50
☐	10527	THE KNAVE OF DIAMONDS by Ethel M. Dell	$1.50
☐	10506	A SAFETY MATCH by Ian Hay	$1.50
☐	10498	HIS HOUR by Elinor Glyn	$1.50
☐	11465	GREATHEART by Ethel M. Dell	$1.50
☐	11048	THE VICISSITUDES OF EVANGELINE by Elinor Glyn	$1.50
☐	11369	THE BARS OF IRON by Ethel M. Dell	$1.50
☐	11370	MAN AND MAID by Elinor Glyn	$1.50
☐	11391	THE SONS OF THE SHEIK by E. M. Hull	$1.50
☐	11376	SIX DAYS by Elinor Glyn	$1.50
☐	11466	RAINBOW IN THE SPRAY by Pamela Wayne	$1.50
☐	11467	THE GREAT MOMENT by Elinor Glyn	$1.50
☐	11560	CHARLES REX by Ethel M. Dell	$1.50
☐	11816	THE PRICE OF THINGS by Elinor Glyn	$1.50

Buy them at your local bookstore or use this handy coupon:

Bantam Book Catalog

Here's your up-to-the-minute listing of every book currently available from Bantam.

This easy-to-use catalog is divided into categories and contains over 1400 titles by your favorite authors.

So don't delay—take advantage of this special opportunity to increase your reading pleasure.

Just send us your name and address and 25¢ (to help defray postage and handling costs).